HOME TO STAY

THE LONG ROAD HOME

MARYANN JORDAN

Home to Stay (Long Road Home Series) Copyright 2021

Cover design by: Cat Johnson

ISBN ebook: 978-1-947214-82-8

ISBN: print: 978-1-947214-83-5

❧ Created with Vellum

Rain slammed against the windows of the Atlanta International Airport terminal, the erratic pelting indicative of the oncoming hurricane. John Roster shifted on the seat, twisting his head to look at the board over their gate's arrival and departure desk. *Flight still listed as leaving on time.* The gate personnel were huddled, their conversation muted, but the one doing the most talking gestured wildly with her hands, indicating a heightened sense of urgency... or she just liked being in charge and enjoyed her position of authority.

A little boy was standing next to the window, his palms splayed out in front of him, his nose pressed to the glass, his eyes wide as the sprays of water bounced on the other side. The wind picked up and a weary-eyed woman appeared, hustling the child back to a seat, toys spread out on the floor in front of him.

"We're never going to make our connection to Orlando."

"Like I don't know that? Spend a fortune for Disney because you just had to have a *destination* wedding. Christ, I wanted Vegas, something adult. But no, you claimed you had to have Mickey and Minnie at the ceremony."

"This storm isn't my fault..."

Bored with the argument coming from the soon-to-be-married-and-probably-soon-to-be-divorced couple behind him, John lifted his hand to rub his eyes, then halted. While he doubted the motion would hurt, his left eye was still sensitive after surgery.

Casting his gaze around at the other nearby gates, the obviously heightened nerves of his fellow travelers were evident. Shoulders slumped, pulled down from the weight of heavy bags as well as weather concerns. Parents snapped at children. Couples snapped at each other. Customers snapped at the airline representatives standing behind the armor of the desk.

Women marching in heels creating a staccato noise in the background along with men dressed for business meetings, their ties loosened and suit jackets abandoned, paced the floor with their cell phones glued to their ears as they shot glances out the window as though glares or prayers could keep Hurricane Helen at bay.

The TV mounted overhead blared about the impending hurricane, the screen filled with meteorologists standing in thin rain jackets, their hoods blown back and wet hair plastered to their foreheads, cautioning everyone to stay inside as the wild winds whipped about them. *If they listened to their own advice, they'd be out of this fuckin' storm.*

John sighed and stretched, the popping in his vertebrae probably heard by others. Without preamble, a voice suddenly sounded on the intercom, resonating throughout the airport.

"Ladies and gentlemen, Atlanta International Airport regrets to inform you that all flights are now canceled coming in and going out of the greater Atlanta region. The hurricane's winds have reached a level that deems airline travel impossible at this time. If you are already through security, please speak to your airline representative at your gate concerning transportation into Atlanta, hotel accommodations, and rescheduling flight arrangements. We thank you for your patience and cooperation."

A collective groan rose into the air, quickly followed by mumbles, cursing, and the sound of people standing quickly as they gathered their belongings.

John stood but walked in the opposite direction. There was no reason to join the crowd around the airline desk at the gate. He swung his backpack over his shoulder and started down the hall. Stopping in front of an airport map, he scanned the legend.

"Can I help you?"

He startled, cursing lightly, having not seen anyone approach. Turning to his left, he saw an elderly man in a red vest, AIA embroidered over the left chest. "I was looking for the USO."

"It's right over there," the man said, tapping his forefinger on the map. "You're in luck. You're already in the Domestic Terminal. You go outside of security, and it's on level three. If you've got bags, you'll have to claim them and recheck them before you can fly out on your rescheduled flight."

John dipped his chin in acknowledgment and started to turn away.

"Thank you for your service, young man."

Swallowing a snort, he dipped his chin a second time. *Young man. Might be compared to him, but damn, I feel old.* Pushing those thoughts to the side, he made his way past security to the baggage claim. The area was packed, and directions continually changed as the LED signs flashed different carousel numbers for different flights. The grumblings were turning mutinous as people pushed and crowded, each sure that they needed to be the first to grab their bags.

He waited, seeing his bags but knowing they'd make the next turn. Sure enough, after more thwarted travelers had left with their bags safely ensconced in their grip or cart, he stepped up, hefting his off the carousel and onto his shoulder.

Eschewing the escalator, he took the stairs, his heavy load not slowing him down. Once on the third level, he followed the signs and stepped through the doorway of the USO. As the glass doors slid closed behind him, he sighed, both in relief and gratitude.

Coming from the right, a woman approached, her white shirt in stark contrast to the bright red apron with the letters USO embroidered across the front. Her dark brown hair swung just above her shoulders as she walked directly up to him, her smile wide.

"Hello! Welcome to the USO! I'm so glad you found us."

Her warm smile was welcome, indeed. "Thank you, ma'am. John Roster. U.S. Army."

"Oh, I'm Blessing." She laughed, her eyes twinkling. "That's my name, not my profession."

Not sure what to say to that, he remained silent.

"Blessing Collier. Now, I just need you to sign in here at the desk, and then I'll show you around. We usually close at nine, but with the storm and flights canceled, we'll stay open all night. I confess we've got quite a crowd, but there's always room here to be found."

"I appreciate it, ma'am—"

"Oh, you can call me Blessing."

After completing the sign-in procedures, he followed her down a hall painted red, white, and blue. She waved her hand to the side toward a large shelving unit that was overflowing with bags, duffels, suitcases, and even strollers parked next to it. "I know we're packed right now. You can just set your bag next to the wall so that no one trips over it."

He followed her instructions, glancing into a room with children sleeping on pallets with their parents slumped nearby in the cushioned sofas and chairs. Another room held uniformed men and women asleep on the floor with their backpacks tucked underneath their heads for pillows.

Remaining silent, he turned his attention back to Blessing, whose smile indicated she was unfazed and unflustered with the spillover. "As you can see, we adapt to whatever we need to."

Her soft laughter was gentle after the crowd at the gate. The tension eased from his shoulders slightly.

"Are you on leave?"

"Discharged. Medical."

Her gaze moved to his face, settling on the redness around his left eye. "Ah… your vision. I'm so sorry."

Blinking, his hands twitched, fighting the desire to fist them in frustration as he thought of his limited sight.

Plowing ahead as though the air between them had not grown thick, she patted his arm. "Where are you heading?"

"M…" He cleared his throat. "Maine."

Her smile widened. "I should have guessed. So stalwart." She lifted her gaze to the ceiling, her brow furrowed. "Ah, yes… 'Should fate unkind send us to roam, the scent of the fragrant pines, and the tang of the salty sea will call us home.'" She chuckled, her shoulders lifting with her mirth. "The state song of Maine, as I'm sure you know."

He swallowed deeply, an unfamiliar ache building in his chest. *Christ, I must be more tired than I thought.* "Yes, ma'am. Well, if you'll just show me where I should bunk down."

She turned and walked down another hall, leaving him to follow in her wake. Looking over her shoulder, she waved to the left. "Showers and toilets are there. And back where we came from is food. Our staff is preparing more for those of you just getting here. Of course, breakfast will be served starting at six a.m. I'm taking you somewhere special. We call it the library. There are others in there like you."

His head tilted to the side. "Like me?"

Soft, lilting laughter met his ears. "Searching. Others who are traveling right now, heading home or somewhere, but searching like you. You know, we all have blinders on in one way or another."

Before he had a chance to question her more, she patted his arm and turned, ushering him through a doorway. He glanced around, surprise hitting him as they stepped into a smaller lounge, plush leather sofas facing each other with a recliner against the wall. Three other men were already slouched on the deep cushions. They looked up as Blessing approached, all three sitting up straighter.

"This is John Roster, Army. And may I present Jaxson Adams, also Army."

Jaxson appeared younger until he stood stiffly, a wince replacing the scowl etched onto his face. They clasped hands as Jaxson said, "Good to meet you. Where are you stationed?"

"I'm out now. Medical discharge."

Jaxson's eyes widened slightly before his gaze landed on the puckered skin near his eye. "Sorry, man. Me, too."

A bit more of the tension he'd held in his shoulders

lifted, but he hated it'd taken another soldier's condition for that to happen.

Blessing stepped over to the next man, who was now standing nearby. "And this is Sebastian Durand. Navy. He's on vacation, heading to his home in Louisiana."

They clasped hands as well, and Sebastian smiled in greeting. "Vacation… leave… hell, probably cleaning up from this storm."

John nodded, the soft Cajun accent reminding him of a few of his Louisiana buddies. "Hope you can find some time to relax."

"And over here is Kyle Jones, also Navy. Heading home to the Appalachians." Blessing clasped her hands in front of her and sighed, a smile curving her lips. "The mountains are so lovely. So peaceful."

Kyle had his foot resting on the coffee table, a cumbersome medical walking boot extended. He slid forward to stand, halting when John reached over and offered his hand.

"Don't get up, man. Keep the load off that leg."

Kyle nodded, relief flooding his features, although John was sure the other man would have rather no one noticed his discomfort. "Thanks. I couldn't believe what a clusterfuck—" He blushed, glancing over at Blessing. "Sorry, ma'am."

She waved away his apology, her ever-present smile firmly in place. "My goodness, I think that's exactly the right description for a crowded airport that gets shut down." She cast her gaze around the room. "Well, I'll leave you gentlemen to rest." With that, she turned and started to walk out the door, stopping at John, her hand gently on his arm. "You know, I have a feeling that you're not looking forward to your return to Maine. Perhaps it's not so much what Maine can do for you but what you can repay."

Blinking, he stared down at her, his brows raised to his forehead. "I'm sorry, I don't understand."

"Find some way to repay the kindness that someone has shown to you. Gratitude goes a long way to helping us find our own happiness." With that, she patted his arm again and left the room.

He stared at the empty doorway, her words swirling inside, adding to the confusion and fatigue pulling at him.

"She's an odd one. Real nice, but a bit odd." Sebastian's words rang true, and John walked over to the sofas, settling into a space next to him with Jaxson and Kyle across from them.

Kyle shook his head. "She's got a weird vibe about her, almost like she knows what's going on before being told."

"She took one look at my face and knew why I was getting out." John lifted his hand, his fingers grazing over the scar by his left eye. Seeing the others' gazes following his hand, he shrugged. "Shrapnel. Lucky I'm not blind, but I lost my peripheral vision on this side." He snorted. "Not bad and yet bad enough."

"What did you do?" Jaxson asked, the leather squeaking as he shifted in his seat.

"Special Forces. Engineer Sergeant."

9

Kyle grinned. "You can build it and demolish it."

He chuckled, the first true sound of mirth that had left his lips in days. "Yeah, that's about the long and short of it." His gaze dropped to the boot again. "You going back in?"

Kyle's short-lived grin was replaced with another scowl. "Don't know. We'll see how the recuperation goes. No room for a gimp with my SEAL team. I may have to decide between paper-pusher and getting out."

"Fuck, man." John understood Kyle's frustration, seeing it mirrored on his own face every day.

"No paper-pushing for a has-been heavy equipment mechanic."

John shifted his gaze to Jaxson, nodding slowly. He opened his mouth, then snapped it shut again. *Who the hell am I to offer words of... what? Condolences? Like that'd be appreciated.* Instead, he simply nodded his under-standing.

"What about you?" Sebastian asked.

Shaking his head, he sighed. "Don't know. Got out and heading back home, for whatever that's worth." He rarely talked about himself to strangers, but sitting on the deep cushions in the comfort of the library, the sounds of the storm raging outside far away and only the three other men as company, he relaxed. "I was an Army brat. Mom took off when I was a kid. When Dad deployed, I stayed with my grandparents in their little house on the coast of Maine. One day, men in uniform came and that was that. Dad had been killed in an acci-dent. Died with his boots on, and believe me, that's how he wanted to go. Spent the rest of my growing-up years with my grandparents. Gramps is still there, and I've got nowhere else to go."

"At least there's home," Jaxson said, his glower less threatening. "Thank God for that."

Soon, Blessing escorted another man into the room. Tall, fit, he had an air of confidence about him. "Gentlemen, this is Air Force Chief Master Sergeant Cameron Freeland. May I introduce you to John Roster, Army."

John took to his feet. "Sir."

Cameron shook his hand, telling him to skip the formalities. After meeting the others, they took seats again, each giving their short story along with their introduction. Cam had taken the recliner to John's left, forcing him to turn his head more fully to keep the man in his sights as they spoke. Cam's gaze narrowed for a few seconds, landing on the scarring before giving an almost imperceptible nod.

"Medical?" Cam asked.

Nodding, he repeated what he'd told the others. "Eighteen C, Special Forces. Lost my peripheral vision with flying debris on our last mission. Surgery saved my sight but not enough. Had four more years to retirement."

Cam talked to all of them about finding new possibilities in the civilian world, but a headache was making it hard to concentrate. Reaching inside his backpack for aspirin, his fingers landed on a packet of paper. He pulled out a letter, the envelope folded and worn. His mind was so focused on the contents, he almost missed Jaxson's question. Looking up, he found all four men staring at him.

"Got letters from a bunch of kids in a school near home. They got my name from the American Legion my grandfather goes to when they wanted a local serviceperson to write to." He shrugged. "It wasn't too bad. Kind of made some of the shit days better."

Jaxson held his gaze, lifting his eyebrow. "Hell, go by and see them when you get home. They'd get a kick out of it."

"You think?"

"We had a couple of servicemen come by for career day when I was in high school. Thought it was the best fuckin' job anyone could ever want."

The idea of visiting a school with a bunch of little kids held no appeal, but he just nodded as Blessing's words moved through his mind. *"Find some way to repay the kindness that someone has shown to you. Gratitude goes a long way to helping us find our own happiness."*

———

John was finally on his way to his departure gate, the atmosphere around him almost manic as passengers hustled along, as anxious as he was to be out of the terminal. Sensing someone's presence just to his left, he jerked his head around to see Cam walking beside him.

"Damn, didn't mean to spook you."

"No worries. Still getting used to limited vision on that side."

"Gotcha. You heading to B terminal?"

"I am." John continued walking with Cam as they

weaved in and out of the crowd, sometimes feeling like a salmon swimming against the stream.

"Me, too. What time is your flight?"

"Not until ten-thirty. I figured I'd camp out at Gate B-24 until my flight was called." The closer they got to the gates the tighter the crowd was, and he thought of Jaxson struggling with his crutches. "Damn, Jaxson is going to have a time getting to his gate."

Cam nodded to a restaurant on the concourse. "Let's stop here. I'll buy breakfast."

John hesitated, but Cam convinced him when he reminded him that they still had three hours before they'd board. Plus, the idea of food and hot coffee was more than enough invitation. Once at a table, Cam leaned back in his seat. "So, home is Maine?"

"Yeah, just my Gramps, but it's the only home I have." As soon as his coffee came, he began digging into his backpack, pulling out a few things until his fingers landed on the ibuprofen. Popping a couple of pills with the hot coffee, he swallowed.

Cam's attention landed on the back of envelopes John had taken out of his backpack. "Mind if I take a look at them?"

John shrugged and handed over one of the envelopes.

Cam slid the folded piece of paper out and began reading, chuckling at the child's letter and picture. Looking up, Cam said, "You said last night these helped you get through some shit days."

John's fingers landed on the stack of envelopes, lightly touching them. "Yeah. Kids are cool."

Cam talked for a few minutes about coaching baseball at Ramstein and it hit John that he'd spent little time in the presence of children. Their conversation moved to their employment chances now that they were out of the service.

"I've been looking for different security firms, but Blessing gave me a lead to chase down."

John mulled over what he said as he silently ate, then curiosity got the best of him. "Why security firm?"

"Military people are in demand for private security. They're looking for disciplined people, and to tell the truth, everything I know about investigations can be taught to a person willing to learn. The biggest thing is attention to detail. Finding significant inconsistencies, for one. Like the same stories from multiple points of view."

John halted his eating, his mind turning over what Cam was saying. "Explain that."

Cam began explaining some of the basics of understanding how people see the same situation through their own eyes, recalling their own memories. Fascinated, John asked, "Where did you learn this?"

"I went to the FBI Academy and they had a guest lecturer who spoke on questioning witnesses and how to talk to people we suspect aligned. It was interesting."

"Sounds like it." By then, the two men had finished their breakfast, both sighing in contentment. "Thanks for breakfast and the talk."

John stood, and Cam lifted his cup of coffee. "Safe travels. If you need anything, man, throw me a text or an email." He handed John a card with his contact information.

With a chin lift and a wave, John headed toward his gate. He still had no idea what kind of work he might be able to find but figured he had some time. After all, he had no idea what *home* would be when he got there. But just like with the kids' letters, he owed Gramps a great deal and figured it was time he repaid that kindness.

2

The SUV rumbled along the coastal highway. It was only a rental from the Portland Airport, but the last thing John had wanted when he finally arrived in Maine was an ordinary midsize sedan. The pickup truck he'd driven between missions had been his pride and joy, but he'd sold it when he left North Carolina. Now, with one hand on the bottom of the steering wheel and the other wrist resting on top, he appreciated the handling and decided this was the next vehicle he'd purchase as soon as he was settled.

Settled. Whatever the hell that means. Settling implied having a place to go home to every evening. Settling implied having a steady job. Settling implied he'd know what he was going to do the next day instead of waiting to see what mission came down the pike.

Following the curves of the road, he snorted. Truth was he hadn't been settled in years, even though he'd considered his team to be his job, his family, and his home. Now, with all that gone, he had no idea what *settled* meant anymore.

Rounding another curve, the ocean came into view and all thoughts of his vehicle or settling left his mind. Sucking in a quick breath as an ache pierced the left side of his chest, he was grateful to see a place to pull off to the side of the road. Parking, he shut down the engine and climbed out, walking around the front. His gaze stayed pinned to the coastal view, so different from many other places that peered out over the Atlantic Ocean. Leaning his back against the side of the SUV, he stared, willing his body to drag in enough oxygen to keep him upright. Clean, crisp air filled his lungs, and the scent of ocean spray mixed with spruce and pine met his senses.

He'd traveled the world, telling himself that home was wherever he lay his head. Staring out at the waves crashing upon the huge rocks of the coast, the blue sky in stark contrast to the deep green forests, he sucked in another deep breath, a sense of peace easing the tension that had filled his neck and shoulders. Home was still a nebulous concept, but at least this was familiar.

Lifting his chin, he allowed the bright sun's rays to warm his face against the spring chill. North Carolina was already warm and muggy this time of year, but Maine was a cool, refreshing balm. Having been stuck in the Atlanta airport for almost thirty hours, it was nice to be outdoors again. Although his time there had not been unbearable. As he cast his mind back to those hours, he had to admit the layover had been good. Blessing had not brought anyone else into the library, so in between snatches of sleep and decent food, he'd continued to converse with Cam, Jaxson, Kyle, and Sebastian. Never one for conversation with strangers, he'd found a simple camaraderie with the other men much like him. They'd even gone so far as to trade cell phone numbers, something he would've scoffed at before their time at the USO.

Another vehicle approached, pulling off to the side of the road near him, a vacationing family spilling from the sides of the minivan. With the quiet reverie broken, he climbed back into the SUV and pulled out onto the coastal road. He passed by several massive million-dollar homes perched on the rocky coastline. Another snort escaped as he thought of his grandparents' house. The house he'd spent years in might have a million-dollar view but was a small, somewhat ramshackle house that his grandfather had barely kept up after his grandmother passed. Some would've been surprised that his grandfather wouldn't have taken the offers that came in for the land around it, but John knew Gramps would never give up that little slice of the Maine coast.

The road turned through thick forests, tall trees on either side. The wall of pine, maple, beech, and oak trees with their branches stretching overhead created a tunnel of green. The area was now familiar, and he turned by the mailbox that was leaning even more than the last time he'd visited. *No reason I can't help the old man out.* He added repairing the mailbox to the start of a mental list of things to do—at least, things to do until he figured out what the hell the next step of his life was going to be.

The winding gravel lane emerged from the woods, exposing a grassy knoll in front of him. And sitting at the end was the gray clapboard house. Three years. That was how long it'd been since he'd laid eyes on the old homestead when he'd come home to visit. He pulled to the front and parked to the side near the garage where the grass had long since been worn down. Climbing from the driver's seat, he grabbed his bags and walked around the back of the SUV toward the door leading into the kitchen.

His grandmother had been gone for almost ten years, but the whitewashed stones that had lined her flower bed still sat in a semicircle by the side of the house. Now faded and more gray than white, the stones brought back memories of a burst of multi-colored blooms from spring to fall. A few blooms now managed to struggle up through the weeds, still offering an occasional dot of red or yellow.

He lifted his hand to knock, then hesitated as more memories washed over him. Letting out a deep breath, he rapped his knuckles on the wooden doorframe. Turning the old, rusty knob, he pushed the door open and stepped inside. The pale yellow walls of the kitchen appeared even more faded, the bright curtains his grandmother had hung long since taken down. A frying pan coated in grease sat on the old stovetop and the scent of strong coffee still filled the room. A few dishes sat soaking in water in the sink, and any remnants of dishwashing bubbles had disappeared.

An oak table sat near the back of the kitchen, the top scarred and worn. He remembered his grandmother telling him that the table was a wedding present from her family. She would scrub it daily, polishing it often, keeping it clean and bright. Now, crumbs battled with dust to cover the top.

The small house was built long before the open-space concept was developed, and he stepped through the narrow doorway leading to the living room at the front of the house. His gaze landed on his grandfather sitting in an old cracked-vinyl recliner, the small flat-screen TV blaring in the corner. His hair was now white, there was less of it, and what was on top stood straight up. His wrinkled clothes appeared clean, but he still had a napkin tucked into the neck of his shirt and draped over his chest. A small tray sat next to him, a now-empty plate resting on top.

As the grey eyes in the weather-lined face looked up at him, John's heart stuttered slightly, and he dipped his chin in a low-voiced greeting. "Gramps."

His grandfather narrowed his eyes before snapping the recliner down, his feet thumping onto the wooden floor. "Huh. Well, boy, you're back." The gravel in his voice gave evidence that he'd probably not spoken yet today... or maybe several days if he'd had no visitors.

John's lips twitched. "Yes, sir, I am."

Gramps' gaze started at John's head and dropped to his booted feet, then slid to the side where the bags had been deposited. As his head lifted again, his gaze landed on the scar by John's eye, and he tilted his head to the side. "You visitin' or home to stay?"

Swallowing deeply, John hesitated. The answer was on the tip of his tongue and yet so difficult to produce. "Home…" He cleared his throat. "I'm home to stay."

Silence crept into the room, but he held his grandfather's steady gaze, not releasing his breath until the older man's head nodded.

"Well, good." Gramps placed his hands on the arms of his chair and pushed himself to standing. Stooped, his tall frame was diminished but still wiry. He walked toward the kitchen but stopped right beside John and placed a rheumatic hand on the doorframe. "Room's same as always. Guess you can find your way. Figure we can use a cup of coffee." With that, he disappeared, leaving John standing alone.

Climbing the stairs, John glanced at the few pictures still hanging on the wall from when his grandmother had lovingly filled five-and-dime frames with snapshots or his school pictures. He shook his head at the scrawny-bodied, geeky-faced boy that peered back at him. *"You'll grow into that body, boy. Be just like your dad."* His grandmother's words had given him hope and turned out true. He'd grown into his large hands and feet, his stature working in his favor in the military.

At the top of the stairs, he glanced to the right into his grandfather's bedroom, seeing it unchanged from the last time he was here. Looking over his shoulder, he stared down the steep staircase and wondered if Gramps had difficulty navigating around. *He'd bite my head off if I asked.* Turning toward the left, he moved into the other bedroom, deciding he'd keep an eye out to see how Gramps handled the house.

His lips quirked upward again as he stepped into his

old room. *Yep. Same as always.* The only improvement had been the double bed he'd bought to replace the small twin bed he'd had through high school. Gramps had thought the expense was unnecessary, but his grandmother had heartily approved. *"Rupert, he needs to sleep comfortably when he comes home, so let him have the bed he wants."* She'd covered it with a homemade quilt, and as he stared down at the faded colors, a rush of emotion slammed into him. This was no visit. *I'm really home this time.*

The furnishings consisted of the bed, a chest of drawers with a small mirror hanging on the wall, and a wooden high-back chair in the corner. Now that he thought about it, it was the same type of chair that Gramps insisted on having in his room as well. *"Man's gotta have a place to sit when he puts on his shoes and socks."*

Dumping his bag onto the floor of the small closet, he walked over to the window and peered out at the coastline in the distance. As a child visiting his grandparents, this view held almost magical power to soothe when thoughts of his mom leaving threatened to overwhelm him. As a teenager who was living here after his dad died, this view simply made him desperate to leave, itching to find his own way outside the little Maine town.

Over the years, he'd spent time on many coastlines and always compared them to this view. Now, he wondered how he'd ever look out this window without thinking of all the places he'd been.

"You comin', boy?"

Blinking out of his reverie, he scrubbed his hand

over his face and stretched his back, as usual hearing his vertebrae pop. "Yes, sir. Be right down."

He made his way into the kitchen, finding a freshly poured cup of coffee sitting on the table. Gramps had poured another one for himself and had already taken a seat. Settling into one of the chairs, John took a sip of the hot, strong brew and grinned. "You always knew how to make a hell of a cup of coffee, Gramps."

His grandfather chuckled. "Your grandmother used to chase me out of the kitchen saying I couldn't boil water. But she had to admit that I could make a cup of coffee."

They sipped in silence, his grandfather's fingers sweeping a few of the crumbs on the tabletop to one side. "'Fraid I don't keep the house up as good as she did."

"Don't worry about that, Gramps. I'm home and have nothing but time right now. I figure there's a lot I can do around here." His grandfather held his gaze, and John braced for the question he knew was coming.

"I thought you had a few more years to retirement." Gramps inclined his head toward John's face. "That scar by your eye have something to do with you showing up here, getting out early?"

His forefinger lifted, barely skimming the puckered skin. Sighing heavily, he nodded. "I wasn't ready, but I can't do my job and protect my team if I can't see from one side." The silence remained, something he was used to from his grandfather. He shrugged. "Got a medical discharge. Decent benefits. I can go to the Togus VA Hospital close by when needed."

"You got plans?"

He stalled, taking another sip, then shook his head. "No. Not anything definite. Up until about two months ago, I was fine. Took a hit and the next thing I know I'm in surgery to repair my eye. All went well except for the peripheral vision on that side. Spent my final weeks in North Carolina with most of my team but figured this was home. Guess I couldn't see going anywhere else." He drained his cup, then said, "Thought I'd help out around here while I figure out what I'll do next."

Gramps looked out the window as the sun set and nodded. "Good place to find yourself. Or lose yourself, whichever needs to happen." He pushed himself to standing and clapped John on the shoulder, his bony fingers digging in slightly as he passed by. "See you in the morning, boy."

Leaning back in the chair, John shook his head, a grin playing about his lips. Gramps was a man of few words and most of those came out gruff, but he didn't doubt the old man's affection. Casting his gaze around, he moved to the sink and washed their cups, then he cleaned the frying pan and brought the plate from the living room into the kitchen to wash it as well. Wiping down the table, he grabbed the broom from the corner and swept the floor.

The sun had dipped into the horizon but it was still early. Watching TV held no appeal, so he climbed the stairs and went into his room, already hearing the snores coming from across the hall. Taking a quick shower, he shoved several pillows against the head-board. Grabbing his backpack, he tossed it onto the bed before settling against the pillows. He pulled out the latest novel he had been reading but found it difficult to concentrate. Tossing the book to the side, he reached inside his pack and pulled out the letters from the kids again. Searching through them, he found the one he was looking for—the class picture. Not formal, the kids were centered in a group in the middle of a classroom, an older, silver-haired woman standing to the side, smiling. Flipping the photo over, he read the now-familiar words:

John, the kids wanted to send you a picture so you'd have smiling faces to carry with you.

Ms. Carrington

Ms. Carrington had said that his name came up from the local American Legion, and since the kids wanted to correspond with a local soldier she hoped he was able to accommodate. His teammates had laughed, telling him to man up and write them back. He had no idea what to say. *Hell, I'd never even written my grandparents while serving.* But one letter led to another—and then he'd started looking forward to them. What he'd said to the men he'd talked to in the USO was true. The kids' letters made a few shitty days better.

He climbed from bed and slipped the photo into the edge of the wooden mirror frame before returning the letter back into its envelope and setting the whole pack on his nightstand. Turning out the light, he figured it couldn't hurt to drop by the school sometime to thank the kids and Ms. Carrington. Rolling over, he punched his pillow. *Right after I fix a few things around the house while looking for a job.*

3

"Gramps, I'm headed to the hardware store."

"Again?" His grandfather had just settled into his recliner, trying to stifle a grunt of pain. Looking up, he held John's gaze. "You've been there every day for almost a week, boy."

"Well, maybe if we'd come up with a list of things that need to be done around here, I can get everything I had to buy in one trip."

"Told you you didn't have to keep doing stuff around the house."

He knew his grandfather had a lot of pride and hated there were things he could no longer do. John had been making repairs every day, each one under the guise of *I'm just fixing this a bit* so his grandfather wouldn't feel as though things around the house had begun to deteriorate.

"Hmph. If you're determined to go, don't forget that plumber's wrench. If I'd had that, I could've fixed the leak a long time ago."

Soon, John pulled into the hardware store parking lot, having lost track of the number of times he'd been to the small store in the past week. He'd managed to replace several warped boards on the front porch, tighten the screws on numerous kitchen cabinet doors and drawers, and fix the drip in the bathroom sink. The stair railing leading to the second floor needed tightening, and as his grandfather reminded, a plumber's wrench was needed to work underneath the sink in the kitchen.

Stepping inside the store, he offered a chin lift to Sally, the older woman sitting behind the cash register. She'd been in the same position almost every time he'd visited, finding out everything she could about him, and offering tidbits of advice.

After grabbing the tools and pieces of PVC pipe he needed, he wandered around for a few minutes, trying to think of other jobs that would need to be done so that he could go a day without coming to the store.

"It's a mighty good thing you're doing for your grandpa," Sally called out. "Rupert used to come in all the time. Sometimes, I think he just wanted to chat more than actually buy something. I know he's been mighty lonely without your grandmother, God rest her soul. A better woman I've never known."

John nodded his agreement but remained silent.

"Rupert would have a fit if he knew I was saying this, but the last couple of years, I noticed his rheumatism had gotten worse. He don't like to admit he's got needs, but having you home to fix up the place without making him feel indebted—it's a real gift."

He shrugged, embarrassed at her compliments. "It's nothing, ma'am."

"Told you the other day to call me Sally. Everybody does."

An unbidden grin slipped across his face. "Well, Sally, if you know my grandfather, you know he likes to look over my shoulder to make sure everything is done just the way he'd like it. Don't suppose you have any clue as to what color he'd like the front door painted, do you?"

"Paint it red."

His brow lowered as his chin jerked back. "Red?"

"Yep. I'm not pulling your leg. He once said he'd love to have a white house with a red front door because it would look like a lighthouse."

John turned and headed back to the paint, stopping when he spied a woman walking down the same aisle, her attention on the paint color chips and her arms full of a variety of items. Her head was down so it was impossible to see her face; it was her outfit that grabbed his attention. A faded blue T-shirt with paint splatters was worn under an old pair of purple overalls at least two sizes too large with a rip in one knee and a swipe of white paint across the ass, distinctly looking as though she'd wiped her paint-covered fingers on the material. Her feet were encased in sneakers that at one time might've been white but were now covered in a combination of paint dribbles and dirt.

Her long, dark hair was pulled up haphazardly on top of her head, a bright pink clip attempting to hold the mass in place, but tendrils waved loose. As comical as her appearance was, her face in profile as she turned slightly toward him now snagged his attention. Rosy cheeks, pale complexion with a dusting of freckles. She was muttering to herself as she held up paint chips, attempting to keep the variety of items in her arms. Not close enough to understand everything she said, he managed to capture a few words.

"Too dark. Should be more green. Nope. Ooh, that one is nice."

As he moved closer to the paint chips, she turned, her gaze landing first on his boots, and her chin lifted slowly as her dark eyes moved upward to his face. His body warmed under her perusal. It wouldn't be the first time that a woman had looked at him in appreciation, but her reaction was surprising. She cocked her head to the side as her eyes narrowed, focusing on his face before giving her head a little shake. Suddenly, as though she just realized she was staring, she inhaled sharply, her chest heaving even though it was hard to discern much movement with the large overalls covering her body.

He started to ask if she was all right when she took two steps backward as she turned too close to the shelves full of paint cans. He watched in horror as her right foot slipped out from under her when she tried to correct her balance. Arms windmilling and flying out, the items she'd held so tightly flung in all directions across the floor. His hand snatched out, just managing to grab onto the strap of her coverall. Barely able to keep her ass from hitting the floor, he hauled her up to her feet, his hand still on the strap.

Stunned motionless for a second, her face soon flushed bright red as her mouth opened in a wide burst of laughter. She looked up, then covered her face with her hands and shook her head. "Oh, my God, I can't believe I did that!"

He let go of her coveralls and stared down, fighting the desire to laugh along with her while her gaze now dropped to her items creating a mess all over the floor. Just as he opened his mouth to offer his help, she dropped and flipped over on all fours, scooping her items back into her arms. The overalls may have been too large, but with her on all fours and her ass pointed his way, his body reacted. Giving a mental shake, he chastised his wayward thoughts and bent next to her to help gather the variety of screws, small tools, paint chips, can of primer, and paintbrushes, placing them in a basket he'd snagged from the end of the aisle.

"Miss, are you all right?"

She looked over her shoulder, her face still flame red. "Yes, I just feel foolish. I really should pay better attention and watch where I'm going."

"Here, let me help you."

"Thank you," she said, smiling. Her gaze moved over his face as though trying to place him before shaking her head again.

He wondered if he'd ever seen her before but came up empty. *It's been a long time since I've lived in the area, but I know I would have remembered her.* Standing, he offered his hand, wrapping his fingers around her much smaller ones.

A jolt ran up his arm. She gasped, looking at their

his dad until his death, and he'd come back to Maine for high school.

He continued to stare out the windshield. Additions had been built onto the back and side of the elementary school, and new outdoor play equipment sat inside a fenced area. A larger fence now encompassed the entire area, and prominent signs directing all visitors to enter through the front and check in at the office were visible even from where he sat.

Glancing at his watch, he wondered if this was a good time to visit. Maybe he should go back to Gramps' place and keep working for a few more days. The last couple of weeks had been spent finding multiple tasks to accomplish under the watchful eye of his grandfather, who pretended he was offering the jobs to John just to keep him busy. He snorted, shaking his head. *Gramps can't do the work but wants his hand in things.*

He had replaced most of the planks on the front porch, making sure the steps were secure. The front and back screen doors had been repaired, their hinges oiled and latches now catching when closed. The drip in the upstairs bathroom sink and the leak under the kitchen sink had been halted with a few twists of a plumber's wrench.

In making his way through the old house, he was pleasantly surprised to find that it was in better shape than he'd originally feared. When he expressed this to Gramps, he'd stood fast as his grandfather snapped back. *"You think I'd live in a dump? I'll have you know that this house is as sturdy as the day it was built. Just a few little things needed tweaking, that's all!"*

While he wasn't sure that Gramps' household assessment was entirely correct, he felt better about where they were living now that he'd had a chance to fix some of the most obvious repairs.

The sound of a bell ringing jolted his thoughts back to the task at hand—going inside to visit Ms. Carrington's fifth-grade class. Dreading it, his cheeks puffed as he blew out a tremendous breath. *Man up, Roster. Take one for the team.* He threw open the door. *Yeah, if my team could see me now, cowering outside, terrified of a bunch of ten-year-olds.*

He walked to the front door and pulled it open, surprised to see that it took him directly to a glassed-in vestibule that led him to the front office only. Once inside, there was a long counter with two secretarial desks behind and a hall that allowed him to see several open office doors. A woman sat behind the counter, a smile on her face.

"Hello, may I help you?"

Having expected to just walk in and find the classroom, he blinked, shocked at the obvious security.

"Uh… yes, ma'am. Uh…"

She kept a polite smile on her face, but her gaze flicked over his large frame and her posture stiffened slightly. Not wanting her to be afraid or call the police, he rushed, "I'm here to visit Ms. Carrington's class."

"And your name, please?"

"John. John Roster. Um… Sergeant John Roster."

Her gaze dropped to a computer screen before returning to him. "I'm sorry, I don't see you on the visitor list. Is she expecting you?"

"Uh… no. I'm sorry, ma'am. I didn't know I needed to make arrangements." He turned to leave, torn between gratitude that he could put the visit off and frustration to have to come back another day.

"Wait, please."

At the sound of the authoritative voice, he turned to locate the source. A tall woman walked from the back hall, her clear-eyed gaze taking him in. "I'm the principal, Ms. Trafalgar. You're the soldier that Ms. Carrington's class has been corresponding with, I believe."

"Yes, ma'am."

"I understand you also attended this elementary school?"

"Only for one year, ma'am, when I lived with my grandparents. I did attend the local high school."

Her smile widened, dropping only slightly when her gaze landed on his scar. "Welcome back home, Sergeant Roster. We thank you for your service."

Dipping his chin in acknowledgment, he waited, uncertain.

Ms. Trafalgar looked at the clock on the wall and said, "Ms. Carrington has about thirty minutes until music. I think that her class would be more than excited to meet you in person." She turned to the receptionist. "Would you have him sign in and then call for an escort?"

"Certainly." The receptionist's smile was now just as welcoming. "I just need your driver's license, please. And once I check you in, I'll have you sign the visitor's log."

He handed over his license, surprised a moment

later when she peeled off a sticker that included his photo and license number along with the date, time, and the classroom he was visiting.

"I didn't expect this kind of security," he mumbled. "It's as tight as a military base."

"Oh, I know." She nodded in sympathy. "But schools nowadays have to be so careful."

After a moment, he looked over his shoulder as Ms. Carrington walked through the door, recognizing her from the photograph. Grey hair, round cheeks, huge smile.

She beamed, her eyes twinkling as she clapped her hands. "Oh, Sergeant Roster, what a treat. Please come with me."

He offered a slight smile and followed dutifully as they made their way down the brightly colored hall, the walls covered with the artwork of the students.

"The students will be so excited. We had no idea you were coming."

"I'm sorry, Ms. Carrington. I should have contacted you to see if this was all right."

Her round, rosy-cheeked face whipped around as she looked up at him, her eyes wide. "Oh, but I'm not Ms. Carrington. I'm the class aide, Mrs. Farthingale."

His feet stuttered to a halt, his brow knit. "I'm sorry? But you were in the photograph…"

"Oh, my gracious! I had no idea what photograph Lucy sent!"

"Lucy?"

"Yes, Lucy Carrington. The teacher. She was taking pictures that day, and I was in a few of them. It never occurred to me that you would think I was the teacher. But you'll just love Lucy! She'll be thrilled you're here!"

She latched onto his arm and began walking at a brisk pace, forcing his feet to follow along. "We're on the back hall where the fifth graders are located." She waved her hand in front of them, her silver hair bouncing as she walked. "Here we are!"

Before he had a chance to beat a retreat, the door was opened, the sound of talking children poured out into the hall, and he was thrust inside the classroom, Mrs. Farthingale at his side.

"Ms. Carrington... class... look who has come to visit us! Our very own Sergeant Roster!"

The room fell silent, and John swallowed deeply as he peered down at the room filled with small desks, small chairs, and small people. *Christ, what have I gotten myself into?*

Hating the black space to the left, he swung his head around to peruse the whole room. A teacher's desk was in the corner and a dark-haired, petite woman stood staring back, her open-mouthed, wide-eyed expression capturing his attention. Her hair was neatly pulled back instead of clipped to the top of her head. Her skirt and blouse were bright colors but weren't covered in paint splotches. Still, he recognized her instantly.

"You?"

"You!"

They spoke at the same time, but she was the first to continue. "You're *John*? I mean Sergeant Roster?"

Stunned to see the woman from the hardware store,

albeit much more professionally attired, he nodded, his head jerking with the motion.

She hurried around the desk toward him, her pink lips curved upward and warm brown eyes pinned on his face. Once again, she didn't focus on his scar but instead held his gaze. "Oh, my… I had no idea… I didn't know… but when I saw you in the hardware store, there was something so familiar about you. But your hair is longer, and your beard is shorter." Sighing, she blushed. "Oh, I'm blabbing again."

Mrs. Farthingale swooped over, hands clasped in front of her. "Isn't this a lovely surprise? And he thought I was the teacher! Well, I must head over to Mr. Pritchett's class. His substitute is having such a hard time. I'll talk to you later!"

They both turned and watched as the aide left the room, barely aware the students were staring at them.

"She talks in exclamation points."

His brow lowered and he turned to face Lucy, not having a clue what to say to her odd pronouncement.

She blushed, shaking her head. "Mrs. Farthingale. I always imagine that she must punctuate all her sentences with exclamation points when she talks. Or, at least, her enthusiasm appears that way to me."

Understanding dawned, and he grinned. "Yes, ma'am. I know what you mean."

"Oh, please, call me Lucy." She glanced toward the class and scrunched her mouth to the side before turning her attention back to him. "Well, here it's best if you call me Ms. Carrington." She glanced up at the clock, her smile falling. "Oh, dear, we only have ten minutes until the class has to report to the music teacher."

"That's all right, ma— Uh, Ms. Carrington. I just dropped by to say thanks for the letters."

"No, no," the children clambered. "We want to talk to him!"

Lucy held up her hand and her brow lifted, shifting her expression from the smiling woman he'd encountered at the store to one who had complete control. Without her saying a word, the class immediately quieted. He was impressed but knew if he'd had a teacher that was as beautiful as her when he was that age, he'd have obeyed, too.

"We'll use the next ten minutes wisely if you cooperate, and then we'll have him come back when we have more time to have a lovely talk with Sergeant Roster."

As though on cue, the kids immediately found their desks, sat down, and quieted, even the ones he instantly discerned would generally be rowdier. He followed her to the front of the classroom where she faced the children. "As you all now know, this is Sergeant Roster, the soldier that we've written to this year, and who has been so gracious to write us back when he was able. We have very little time right now for questions, but hopefully, he'll be able to fit in another visit before he has to return to the service."

It was on the tip of his tongue to let her know that he wouldn't be going back but he said nothing. *That would just open up questions for the kids that I don't want to answer right now.* He nodded. "I can arrange to come back easily."

Her worried expression fled, and it struck him how glad he was that he'd been able to give her an answer that brought about such a beautiful smile. Turning to look toward the kids, he was more relaxed now that he saw their eager faces. "I'm glad to have the opportunity to thank you for writing to me. It was a real surprise when I got the first letter, and I wasn't sure that I had anything to say. But I was grateful as the letters kept coming, giving me a little piece of home no matter where I was."

"Did you miss home?"

The question came from a girl in the front row, her blue eyes sharp behind her glasses as she held his gaze.

"Yes, of course. I had moved around a lot as a kid, but this was where I made some of my best memories, including my teenage years, so... yeah. I missed Maine."

Other hands lifted into the air, and for a few seconds his breath caught in his lungs, hating to talk about himself, but Lucy's soft voice cut through his panic.

"Okay, class, you need to thank Sergeant Roster for dropping by and then form a line. Mrs. Carswell will be here momentarily."

With efficiency worthy of military precision, she had the class lined up at the door and watched as they were escorted down the hall. Before he could blink, he was alone with her. But seeing her standing in front of him, her dark eyes peering up and her lips curved, he hated that he had no excuse to stay.

"You shaved."

He blinked, lifting his hand to his clean-shaven face. "Uh, yes."

After scribbling, she turned, and he was glad his gaze had lifted from her ass. She smiled as she approached, handing him her number.

"As soon as you know your schedule, please, call and we can set up a return visit."

He looked down at the slip of paper, her phone number printed neatly underneath her name. A flash of memory ran through his mind of a girl in high school slipping him a note with her phone number. Giving his head a little shake, he wondered what it was about being back in the school building that sent the mind to wander along paths from long ago.

"Or... If you'd rather not..."

His gaze shot from the piece of paper to her face, doubt clouding her bright eyes. Now shaking his head vehemently, he rushed, "Sorry, no, I want to. It seems that being back in the school is playing tricks on my mind. But I can call you, although the truth of the matter is... well, my schedule is very open."

She tilted her head to the side, curiosity in her eyes.

Sighing, he scrubbed his hand over the back of his head, his fingers squeezing his neck. "I'm out of the Army. Medical discharge."

Her gaze moved to his scar before immediately returning to his eyes. "Oh, John, I'm so sorry."

He shrugged. "It is what it is."

Her pink lips opened as though to speak, then shut, and she simply nodded instead. "Are you going to stay in the area?"

"Yes. My grandfather is here. He needs some help around the house, so I figure I'll stay and make sure he's okay. I've got nothing else going on right now." As soon as those words left his mouth, he wondered what the hell had gotten into him. *Yep, unemployed loser here. That sounds impressive.*

Her chin dropped, her eyes lowering for a moment, and he wondered what she was thinking. She didn't make him wait long before she reached out and touched his arm again.

"Are you still willing to talk to the class? You can talk about the military if you want, but I'd so much rather you talk to them about your life and what you're doing now."

He jerked slightly. "Now? But I don't understand."

"These children are only ten, but it's never too young for them to learn that life doesn't always hand them what they want. Or that sometimes plans have to change. I think it would be good for them to see a confident soldier but also see someone who is having to forge a new direction." She sucked in her lips, pressing them tightly together, another blush rising over her cheeks. "Wow, I'm sorry. That was terribly forward of me to assume you'd want to talk about any of this."

"No," he rushed, wanting to erase her embarrassment. "You're right. They're not too young to know that... well, that life changes. But I'm not so good at talking about myself."

Her smile removed the crinkle that had formed between her brows. "You'll be wonderful, I'm sure."

The sound of children's voices in the hall met his ears, and he slipped the paper with her number into his pocket. "So, I'll give you a call, but seriously, I can come almost any time."

"I'll look forward to hearing from you." She glanced up at the clock on the wall. "I'll walk you out on my way to pick up my class."

He nodded, glad to have another few minutes in her company, although as they walked down the hall he couldn't think of anything to say. Inwardly cursing at how quickly they reached the office, he turned and forced out some words. "It was nice to meet you, Ms. Carrington." *Smooth, Roster. Real smooth.*

Her smile widened, and he could swear the hallway brightened. She once again placed her hand on his arm, her fingers twitching slightly over his muscles.

"John, you have no idea how glad I am you came today. It was... I mean... it is so nice to meet you, too. It's wonderful to have you back safely. I've thought of you often... well, your safety. Yes, I thought of your safety often." She shook her head and laughed, her cheeks rosy once again. With a final squeeze on his arm, she turned.

After watching her walk back toward her classroom, he headed outside to the parking lot and climbed into his vehicle, his heart lighter than it had been in months.

5

Lucy gripped the windowsill, her knuckles white as she watched John climb into his vehicle in the school parking lot. Not realizing she was holding her breath, it finally rushed out, the moisture clouding the glass. Jerking to the side so she wouldn't miss a second of seeing him, she finally loosened her grip as he drove out of sight. *John. Sergeant John Roster. Here. Right in front of me. Oh, God, and I splattered myself onto the floor right in front of him the other night in the store.*

She tried to remember exactly how bad that scene was, and her face grew hotter at the memory. *Staring stupidly at him because I thought he looked like John but knew it couldn't possibly be him. He had to grab me by my overalls. My overalls?* She banged her forehead against the glass window, her eyes now closed as mortification rushed through her. *Oh, my God, he saw me in all my messy glory. And then I dropped all my items and had to scramble on all fours... wait, was my ass in his face as he bent down to help me? Oh, God, I think it was!*

She banged her head on the glass window again. No one knew the nights she'd lain awake, a copy of the photograph he'd sent of him and his buddies resting on her nightstand, propped up against the lamp so it was clearly visible when she opened her eyes each morning for the past eight months. *I'm such a dork.*

In the picture, he'd had short hair, a beard, his sunglasses pushed up on top of his head, and his arms slung around some of the other men. While the others smiled widely, his smile had been reserved, the slight curving of his lips presenting a more serious expression than his teammates with their devil-may-care grins. At least, that's how it appeared to her. And she'd looked at the picture enough to have every nuance analyzed and memorized.

"Handsome, isn't he?"

She jumped, her hand landing on her chest as she whirled around. Mrs. Farthingale stood just behind her, a smile on her lips and a twinkle in her eyes.

"Oh, Charlotte, you scared me!"

"I'm not surprised. You were rather focused on the delicious Sergeant Roster."

"No… I was just… I heard it might rain and wondered if I needed my umbrella when I left today."

Charlotte's brow lifted just before her chest bounced as laughter erupted. "Only if it's raining men, my dear."

Another hot blush flooded her face and she turned, looping her hand through the older woman's arm. "Come on, I've embarrassed myself enough for one day."

They headed back to the room in silence until they arrived at her classroom door. Charlotte's eyes bored a hole through the side of Lucy's head and, unable to remain silent, she swiveled around. "What? You might as well say it. I know you're dying to."

"Hmph. I was just thinking that you should invite him to dinner. Nothing like a home-cooked meal for a man who's been in the service and rarely gets such a treat."

Before Lucy had a chance to respond, her class came down the hall from their music lesson and into the room, their chatter all about Sergeant Roster.

"Is he coming back, Ms. Carrington?" The question was hurled from several of the children crowded around.

Clapping her hands, she called them to order, and once seated, announced, "Yes, Sergeant Roster will be coming back. I'll make arrangements, and we can plan something special as a homecoming for him."

The dismissal warning bell rang, indicating they had five minutes before the buses would begin to load. Clapping her hands again, she hustled the children to gather their materials and watched as they lined up at the door.

One of the smaller girls in her class touched her arm.

"Yes, Christina?"

"We could give him a party."

"Nah," Bobby piped up. "I want him to show us how to do push-ups and jump over walls like they do in the commercials."

"When I talk to him, I'll find out what he thinks

would be best, how about that?" she replied, gaining the nods of the others.

Before long, the children had left, her room was ready for the next day, her lesson plans were written on the board, and she was finally in her car. She arrived at home, surprised to have made the trip mostly on autopilot, barely remembering the drive, her mind so full of thoughts of *him*.

Her house was tucked at the end of the lane, not part of a subdivision but not too far away from one that she felt completely alone. Woods surrounded the back of her house, and a small, separate garage sat to the side. Looking at her house, she knew what others, including her family, observed. A small, older cottage with fresh paint on the front but not the sides and back, an over-grown yard, shutters that had been taken down and leaned against the front as they waited for new paint, and a front screen door that was missing the screen. The inside was a litany of projects that needed to be completed also.

Granted, she wasn't trained in construction but was learning as she went, and with each completed project she added to her sense of pride. A cabin in the woods, something she could work on to discover its original charm, was perfect. The fact that the back of her property bordered a tributary that led out through a bay and from there onto the ocean made it even more valuable to her.

She'd been able to afford it on her teacher's salary. *"Not surprising, considering all the work that needs to be done,"* her father had reminded.

Alighting from her small car, she grabbed her school bag and walked to the front door, carefully opening the screenless screen door, wincing as the hinges creaked loudly. Inserting her key into the lock in the wooden front door, she jiggled it numerous times before the key finally turned. Once inside, she headed straight to the kitchen after dropping her bag and shoes by the front door. She'd skipped lunch to finish her lesson plan and thought she might grab takeout on the way home, but her surprise visitor had muddled her thoughts and she was almost home before she remembered to stop anywhere.

She pulled open the refrigerator door with a grin, acknowledging that John's visit was worth not having takeout. She stared inside, discovering few choices and none very exciting. Finally, she grabbed a package of sliced ham, mayonnaise, and a piece of cheese she hoped wasn't moldy. Hastily making a sandwich, she was excited to discover she still had some potato chips that weren't too stale. Squirting a shot of orange-flavored water enhancer into her water glass, she smiled as she thought of the Kool-Aid her mother used to make when she was a little girl.

Sitting at her small table, she ate her sandwich absentmindedly as she opened her phone to the app where she kept notes. She started her grocery list, then switched to a list of items needed at the hardware store.

Her phone vibrated an incoming call and she jumped, her heart leaping until she spied it was from her friend. Answering, she could not keep the disappointment from her voice.

"Wow, you don't sound very excited to hear from me."

"Sorry, Paula," she replied, trying to add a level of brightness to her voice. "I was just thinking about what project to work on this weekend."

"Honey, that dump of a house will always have a project. What's not to work on?"

While the sentiment was true, she bristled. "Well, at least I'll never be bored as long as I have this house to work on." Paula laughed, and Lucy had no problem imagining her friend's eyes rolling.

"Well, I happen to know there's a decent band at Moose's Bar tonight. A couple of beers and hopefully a couple of guys will be just the thing to drag you away from your house."

While at another time that invitation of drinking, dancing, and flirting would've held some appeal, tonight it didn't. "Sorry, I just don't feel like going out tonight."

"That wouldn't happen to have anything to do with the handsome soldier that visited you today, would it?" Paula laughed again. "I thought I'd get a chance to see you at the end of the day, but you left on time and I was stuck in a department meeting." A third-grade teacher at the same school, they'd become friends when Paula moved to the area two years ago.

"I should have known that the news of John's visit would have traveled like wildfire through the faculty."

"Hey, I spend my days with a bunch of eight-year-olds. You've got to give me the lowdown on him!"

"I was surprised, that's for sure. I had no idea he was stateside. We only had a few minutes to talk, but he agreed to come back so that he could have more time with the kids."

"Yeah, but what about spending time with you?"

It was on the tip of her tongue to insist that spending time with John was just for the class' benefit, but Paula knew her better than that. "I gave him my number so that he could let me know when he can come back and arrange a time."

"And you're hoping he'll call just for you."

Lucy sighed. "I won't deny that it would be nice, but I got the feeling from him today that he has a lot of things to figure out in his life. I hardly think I'll be anything more than just a way to visit the class to check something off of his to-do list. Lord knows I certainly understand that."

"Well, if you're not sitting by the phone waiting for him to call, you've got no excuse to deny my attempt to drag you out to Moose's tonight. Just for the music and one beer, okay? Look, since I know your secret crush is home, I won't even insist on you dancing. Just sit and listen to the band and relax after a crazy week. Those shutters that need to be painted will still be there tomorrow."

While going to the bar with Paula was not what had been her plan for the evening, she and Paula had made it a habit to support local indie musicians. "Okay," she gave in. "But I'm driving because I'm only staying for one drink and one set. And I know you. No matter what you say, you'll end up staying longer, especially if you catch the eye of one of the musicians."

Paula laughed and agreed. "Okay, okay. I'll meet you

there in an hour. And I promise you'll have a good time. This band is supposed to be really up-and-coming. It should be epic."

Epic... A flash of John ran through her mind—tall, dark, so gorgeous it almost hurt to believe someone could be so attractive and not seem to know it. And how just a tiny smile from him warmed her heart more than a huge grin from any other man. Now *that* was epic.

Disconnecting, she washed her plate and headed back to her bedroom to change. Maybe a Friday night doing something besides painting shutters would be interesting. *At least not as mortifying as landing on the floor at John's feet in a hardware store.*

John rinsed the dinner dishes while Gramps dried them. He worked patiently, adjusting his movements to his grandfather's slower pace. When the kitchen was put to right, he assumed they'd retire to the living room. Instead, Gramps leaned against the counter and pinned him with a stare.

"Whatcha got planned for this evening?"

John's chin jerked back slightly and he turned fully to face the older man. "Well... nothing."

"Then let's go to Moose's Bar. Gonna meet a friend, and he offered to come to pick me up, but I told him that you were here and could take me."

"Uh... sure." He hadn't been to Moose's Bar in years. Maybe he'd been once or twice on visits back home, but this was the first time Gramps had asked him to go. "Let me change, and I'll be back down."

"Hell, boy, it ain't fancy," Gramps groused.

"Yeah, well, I've sweat enough today to know I reek." He hustled up the steps and jerked off the button-up shirt he'd worn to the school. Balling it up, he tossed it in the laundry basket in the corner. He was surprised Gramps hadn't complained of the smell when he came in. It definitely wasn't the odor from hard-work sweat but nerves. *Hell, missions didn't make me as nervous as I was today.* Reaching into the drawer, he pulled out a clean, dark blue T-shirt and slid it over his head. Shoving his wallet and phone into his pockets, he headed back down the stairs.

It didn't take long to drive to Moose's Bar. One of many bars in the area, it was frequented by old-timers and newcomers alike. He had no doubt it could get rowdy on a Friday night but remembered Gramps had told him that the crotchety owner was a Desert Storm veteran and ran the bar that his father, the original Moose, had started when he'd come back from the Vietnam War.

Pulling into the parking lot, he was surprised at the number of cars. "Has this place gotten more popular?"

Gramps climbed out of the truck and slammed the door. "Bunch of young locals convinced Moose that he should occasionally have musicians come in and play. Who the hell needs to listen to anything but a jukebox playing in the background of a bar?"

They walked to the front, and he held the door open as his grandfather stepped inside. Looking around, John was glad to see that the small band had set up in the back corner, most of the listeners there as well. Other than the musicians, the interior hadn't changed since the last time he was there. The wooden floor was still scuffed and the wooden bar, while clean, had a few more dents.

Before he had a chance to ask about Gramps' friend, his grandfather's face broke into a wide smile and he tossed his hand into the air. Glancing to the side, John spied an older, barrel-chested man, his gunmetal gray hair cut high and tight. He couldn't help but grin as Gramps hustled over to the table. Following along, he was thankful that the other man had snagged a regular table and not a high top, probably in deference to his grandfather. The two older men shook hands and Gramps settled himself into the chair, inclining his head toward the one next to him for John to take. He would have preferred his left side be next to the wall but took the chair offered, knowing he would have to glance to the side more often to make sure he could see everything around.

"Horace, I'd like you to meet my grandson, John. John, this is a good friend of mine, Horace Tiddle."

He reached across the table, taking the man's hand, receiving a firm shake. "Nice to meet you, sir."

Horace laughed and shook his head. "Call me Horace. Sir was for the officers in the military, not me, and now, as a civilian, it just makes me feel old."

"What service?"

"Navy. SEAL."

A chin lift was his acknowledgment of the man's accomplishments, knowing it would be understood.

After ordering their beer, Horace turned his attention to John. "I understand you're recently out of the Army? Special Forces?"

"Yes, sir— Horace." He reached up and touched the scar by his eye, for the first time not feeling self-conscious. "Took some shrapnel, and while surgery saved my sight, I have no peripheral vision on that side. It's kind of like having a black spot always there."

Horace nodded slowly. "I know that's gotta be hard, John. I had injuries but nothing that warranted a medical discharge. Although, I admit at the time I got out my body was feeling every ache and pain."

"I was in sixteen years, so I understand."

A smiling server brought their beer over, and while the band began to play in the background, the three men continued to chat. He discovered that Gramps and Horace had met at the local American Legion Chapter and from their conversation divined that it was not a dying membership.

"It's not a super-active chapter," Horace admitted, "but there are plenty of young men and women who moved into the area or came back home that participate."

John leaned back in his chair, sipping his beer and listening to the music, surprised to discover the band played decent covers and a few originals.

"So, John, what are your plans? Rupert told me you've been working on his place, which I know he's grateful for. But do you have any specific job plans now that you're out of the Army?"

Once again, he found that with Horace he didn't feel the same sense of frustration that he usually did. "I wish I could give you a definitive answer but I don't have one. I'd planned on finishing my years in, and if my body held out, do a few more. I never wanted a desk job, but I'd thought I might go into training others."

Gramps piped up, "I told him that security clearance ought to be worth something. All he learned, all the missions he went on, he can plan, think fast on his feet, smart as a whip."

It was nice to hear the pride in Gramps' voice, and John shook his head and grinned. "Gramps, thanks for the vote of confidence, but I'm not sure I can get a job based on my grandfather's recommendation."

Gramps opened his mouth but his comment was cut short when Horace jumped in. "I work for a company located near here. I have no idea if it's something you're interested in or if they'd be interested in you. But I'd like you to at least meet the boss."

Intrigued, having assumed Horace was leisurely retired, he tilted his head to the side. "What kind of work are you in?"

"I work for a security company. Lighthouse Security and Investigations. They don't advertise for positions. When the boss started his company several years ago, he'd handpicked his employees from various Special Operations, including CIA Special Ops." He chuckled and shook his head, his eyes twinkling. "That's how we found out about it. My wife worked with the boss on a

CIA operation. My wife keeps them on their toes. She's about as close to a grandmother drill sergeant as you can imagine."

John's brows lifted to his forehead at that tidbit of information, then he turned toward his grandfather, who'd adopted a not-so-subtle innocent expression as he tipped his beer up. "Gramps, is this why you were asking me about security the other day?"

"Hmph. I might've mentioned to Horace that you were former Special Forces, back home now."

He battled the sliver of interest that threatened to grow. "Saying I'm not interested would be a lie, Horace, but I don't know anything about the security business. And, with my vision..." He let his last phrase hang out there, not knowing if it would make a difference.

"I wouldn't let that worry you." Horace rubbed his hand over his chin. "Like I said, I have no idea if you are even interested, would be the right fit, or if LSI is looking, but the boss is a good man, former Army Special Forces also, and worth knowing even if you aren't an employee. Hell, not just the boss but all the employees."

Interest flared, and he nodded. "Okay, Horace, I'd like to meet your boss, even if it's just nothing more than to buy him a drink."

Horace slapped his hand onto the table and grinned. "Well, all right. Give me your number, and I'll let him know."

After giving him his contact information, they stood as Horace clapped Gramps on the shoulder. Stepping back, he turned. Blindsided, he was slammed into by a body, instantly followed by the cold rush of beer pouring down his shirt.

"Goddamnit! What the— Lucy?"

Staring up at him was Lucy, dressed in a bright red shirt, her eyes wide, her mouth opened, and a half-empty beer mug in her hand as the rest of it he was now wearing.

6

"Oh, shit!" As the words left her mouth, Lucy barely heard the laughter from the two older men standing nearby.

"Think I'll give Rupert a ride home, John. Nice to meet you, and I'll be in touch," one of them said to John.

The flash of anger in his eyes had now morphed into resignation as he recognized her. He nodded toward the one who spoke before turning back to her.

"Oh, John, I'm so sorry!" She set the mug on the table and grabbed a wad of napkins, dabbing at his shirt in a feckless effort to make the mess a little less messy. All it did was make the tight, now-wet t-shirt stick even more to his sculpted abs and chest. The moisture left her mouth but she managed to keep from grabbing what was left of her beer from the table and chugging it.

His large hands settled over hers, stilling the motion. He unfurled her fingers, pulling the soppy napkins from her grip and tossing them to the table next to the mug.

"I can't believe I did that! I just ran right into you! I was looking down at my feet because I hate to step in sticky places where people have spilled beer. Oh, my God, now that's me. There's a wet place on the floor that's going to become sticky. And I've ruined your shirt. I'll buy you a new one, honest. Just give me your size... well, that's probably an extra-large, isn't it? Not that you're overweight. Just big. Big in a good way. Not that there's a bad way to be big—"

"Lucy."

She stopped babbling, not because John's voice was a loud command but more from a firm desire that she should let him speak. "Yes?"

"It's fine. It's just a T-shirt and beer. Nothing that won't come out in the wash."

"Oh, right. Well, I can wash it for you—"

"There's no need."

His hands still covered hers as they rested on his chest, and the warmth from their touch replaced the shock of their accident. The blue of his T-shirt made his eyes appear stormy gray but not from anger. Need? Desire? *I'm probably imposing my own thoughts on him.* Licking her lips, she glanced around, thankful that no one was paying them any attention. "Oh, your friends have left."

"That was my grandfather and a friend of his who'll take him home."

She sighed, shaking her head. "Oh, you were his ride home, weren't you?"

"It's okay. He'll be just as happy to have his friend driving him home. Anyway, I'm glad to see you."

Her breathing relaxed as it appeared he truly wasn't angry. "I'm glad we met again, too, although the way we met was a bit auspicious."

"You think?" he laughed. He looked around before settling his gaze back on her. "Were you here with anyone... um... special?"

"I'm here with a friend, but from the looks of things, I'm about to get ditched." His body stiffened, the feel of his muscles tightening underneath her fingers.

"I can't imagine anyone ditching you." His voice was a growl, and while she'd read that vocal description in books, she had never actually heard someone growl before. The way his tone vibrated through her body ended in her core, and she decided that he could growl at her any time he wanted. A crinkle had settled between his brows, and she wanted to reach up and smooth it away.

"Well, my girlfriend, Paula, wanted me to hear this band. She goes to lots of concerts and heard this one from Canada at a music festival up there. I was kind of her wingman, and she'll leave with whoever catches her attention." She jerked her head from side to side quickly, adding, "That sounded very uncharitable. We usually have a good time, and truthfully, I don't come out very often. Plus, I drive separately so I can leave whenever I want."

"So, you weren't on a date?"

She laughed, and a little snort slipped out, followed by a blush. "No. I was going to stay at home and paint my shutters, but she convinced me I could do that tomorrow."

"Paint your shutters?"

"Yes. I have a lot of house projects. That's why I was in the hardware store."

"That sounds like me. I've been helping my grandfather around his house. He's the one who suggested we come out tonight." His gaze shifted over to the beer on the table, and he turned back to her. "Can I buy you another beer since that one's half-empty?"

"No. I just went to the bar to have something to do while Paula was flirting with the musician between sets." She scrunched her nose and added, "But the crowd is different tonight. The band seems to draw mostly bikers... big, kind of scary bikers. But Paula's cool. She has no fear, so I guess my wingman duties are over for the night." As soon as the words left her mouth, she inwardly winced. *Damn, why didn't I take him up on buying me a drink? Anything to keep talking to him for a while!*

"Then can I walk you to your car, or would you like to stay and listen to the music some more?"

"If you're leaving, you can walk me to my car, but if you're staying, I'd love to stay with you."

Her breathing eased as she watched the smile curve his lips, hard-won and even more gorgeous than she'd imagined. He placed his hand on the small of her back and guided her through the crowd with his other arm outstretched to keep others from bumping into her. She felt the burn of his fingers through her shirt and battled the desire to plaster her side to his.

The musicians were back from their break, cranking

out the cover songs again. The bikers took up most of the tables and seats, but she followed John as he found a spot against the wall. He leaned back, then bent to whisper into her ear. "I'd let you lean your back against me, but it might smell a bit of beer."

Who cares?! "Oh, no worries. If you have to wash your shirt, there's no reason I can't wash a bit of beer out of mine as well." She shifted her weight and leaned against him, his broad chest the perfect backrest.

His breath warmed her neck as he leaned forward again. "Are you sure your friend is in this crowd?"

She swung her gaze around before spying Paula sitting at a table to the side with a few of the rough-looking bikers. Considering Paula had talked about the band, Lucy was surprised to see the company her friend was keeping. Standing on her tiptoes, she inclined her head toward the table. "That's her over there in the black shirt."

After a moment, Paula looked around and caught Lucy's eye, waving. Leaning over to say something to one of the men at the table, she hopped up and weaved through the crowd, stopping in front of Lucy. "I wondered what happened to you when you didn't come back from getting your beer. I was ready to set you up with one of my friends over there. He was looking forward to meeting you." Paula's gaze shifted upward to John, appreciation sparking in her eyes. "Oh, now I can see why you didn't come back!" She smiled up at him. "I'm Paula."

"John."

Paula's eyes widened and she dropped her gaze back to Lucy. "Your soldier?"

Feeling the blush heat all the way to her hair follicles, Lucy made big eyes at Paula, who appeared to have drunk enough to have loosened her tongue, her inhibitions, and her good sense. "Not *my* soldier, but yes, John is the soldier my class was writing to."

"Well, well, I can see why you—*umph!*" Her words halted as Lucy kicked Paula's ankle.

"I thought you were here for one of the musicians."

Paula glanced to the table behind her and grinned. "They're okay, but I hooked up with one of them when I was in Canada. Honestly, it's the bikers that I'm interested in right now."

John stiffened behind her, tension radiating off his body. Uncertain of the reason, she kept her focus on her friend. "Just be careful. Text me when you leave, and let me know who you're with."

Paula rolled her eyes and patted Lucy's arm. "Yes, Mom." Laughing, she added, "I'll see you on Monday. Nice to meet you, John."

"Same."

The single word rumbled from his chest, and Lucy felt the vibration through her back. Paula made her way back to the table, and Lucy observed as her friend leaned over and spoke to one of the bikers. He swung his head around and glared toward Lucy. Wondering if that's who Paula was hooking up with or was the one who thought he might hook up with her or was just generally grumpy, she leaned further back into John, not wanting more of the biker's attention.

"Do you want to stay and keep an eye on her?" he asked.

She twisted her head around and looked up at him. "I've never had to do that before. She's not really wild, she just likes to have fun. But she's always been safe, and if she's planning on hooking up with someone, she makes sure to snap their license plate and sometimes even the driver's license and text it to me."

"Smart. I wouldn't have pegged her for being that smart based on meeting her tonight."

Brow furrowed, she blinked. "What do you mean by that?"

He shook his head as one of his hands rested on her waist. "I'm sorry. I shouldn't have said that considering I've only known her for about one minute. And she's your friend. It's just that I wouldn't be comfortable with a woman I know sitting down with those men at the table."

Already feeling guilty about her prejudice based on the look of the men and having never felt prejudice against bikers before, she opened her mouth to question John, but he wasn't finished.

"I've got a lot of friends who ride, and I've got no problem with bikers. But I don't like the look of some of those men." Shrugging, he added, "I've got no facts to base that on. Just a gut feeling. But in Special Forces, my gut saved my life more than once, so I trust it."

Sliding her phone out of her pocket, she sent a quick text to Paula reminding her to take a picture if she was going to hook up. She watched as Paula read her text then looked up and grinned, shooting Lucy a thumbs up. "Okay, I feel better now."

"If you're ready, I'll walk you to your car." She nodded, smiling up at him. This time, instead of placing his hand on the small of her back, his fingers skimmed down her arm and linked with hers. He led her through the crowd, and with his size, it was like the parting of the Red Sea. She loved the feel of her hand in his, having dreamed about it for months.

Once outside, the cool air slapped her back into reality. *He's just making sure I'm safe.* She lifted her hand and pointed. "I'm the small car over there, under the light." They walked to her car, and he stood next to it as she clicked the key fob. Turning around, she looked up, finding his attention focused directly on her.

"I know you gave me your phone number, Lucy, but I'd like to give you mine. I'd feel a lot better if I knew you got home safely tonight."

She didn't care what the excuse was but having his phone number made her inner Lucy jump up and down with glee. "That would be perfect," she said, hoping he didn't notice the quiver of excitement in her voice. After keying in his number, he stepped back and waited while she climbed inside. Tossing him a wave and a smile, she started her car. Through her rearview mirror, she could see him standing in the parking lot under the light until she was out of sight.

Once she pulled into her driveway and looked toward her cottage with the front illuminated by a porch light and motion-sensor light, something her dad insisted on, she smiled. For the whole drive, she was on senses overload. The sound of John's rough voice. His quiet but steady presence. The hard planes of his chest against her back. The warm ruffle of his breath against her ear when he bent to speak. The point of his chin resting lightly on her head as she leaned against him. The burn of his fingertips on her back. The electricity jolting up her arm from their linked hands.

Finally, blowing out a breath, she alighted and hustled into her house, the key only sticking momentarily. Once inside, she sent him a text.

Home safely.

Good.

She hesitated. His one-word reply reminded her of his succinct letters she'd read to her class. Taking a chance that he wouldn't mind more, she typed again.

Glad you were there tonight.

Me too.

Okay... is he just being polite? His text came in almost immediately after hers which indicated he was still engaged in the text conversation. Sucking in a quick breath, she decided to continue. *What have I got to lose? My dignity? Not after dumping beer all over him... and in front of his grandfather!*

So sorry about the beer. You were very gracious.

No worries. It meant we met again and I got to spend more time with you.

Once again, her inner Lucy hopped up and down, her fingers continuing to text as a smile raced across her face.

Next time you go to Moose's, let me know. I'll attempt a re-do that's less messy.

How about you come with me sometime?

Flopping down on her sofa, she ignored the adolescent giggle that slipped out.

I'd love to.

Then it's a date. And when do you want me to come to the class?

The thought of typing *'immediately'* hit her mind, but with a shake of her head knew that was ridiculous. Monday would be good but her class would have no time to prepare. Running through the class schedule, she grinned.

How about Wednesday, 2 pm. That will give the class an hour with you, and we'll have snacks.

Perfect. Can I bring anything?

Only yourself.

A moment passed with no other text and she sighed. *I guess that's all for tonight. Or maybe until I see him again.* She tried to tell herself it didn't matter if she was just the teacher and he felt an obligation. Or that he was just a really good guy who made sure she was safe at the bar. Moving into her bedroom, she stripped, then lifted her shirt to her nose, sniffing the faint scent of beer mixed with the woodsy, male scent that was John. Tossing it into the hamper, she shook her head. "God, I'm pathetic," she said aloud. Yawning with fatigue, a five-minute shower was all she allowed. Slipping into sleep shorts and a camisole, she was brushing her teeth when her phone dinged an incoming message. She bolted into the bedroom, then turned and rushed back to the sink to spit and rinse before grabbing her phone from the nightstand.

Sorry. Got home and wanted to check on Gramps.

She typed and erased several texts, worried they might seem too personal, too inquisitive, too intrusive. Finally, she went for simple.

That's nice. As soon as she hit send, she dropped her chin to her chest. "Yep. It's official. I'm pathetic at text flirting... or... whatever we're doing." Another moment passed with no incoming text, and she was afraid she'd bored him to sleep. Sliding under the covers, she lay her head on the pillow, her phone in her hand and her gaze on the photograph propped on her nightstand. When her phone vibrated, she jolted.

So, I come on Wednesday to your class. Can't help but notice that is 5 days away. Seems kind of long.

Heart singing, she grinned, her fingers flying. **Is that too far away?**

Considering I'd like to see you again... yeah.

Her fingers halted over the keyboard. *What to do? Where to meet?* Before she had a chance to decide on a reply, he texted again.

How about dinner on Sunday?

Her heart sank. She had a standing family dinner every Sunday, only to be missed by death or dismemberment according to her mom. **Have a family thing. How about I fix you dinner tomorrow?**

Even better but I should take you out.

Nah... I like to cook. And you can see my cottage. It's a work in progress.

It's a date. Text me time and address.

Perfect. Can't wait.

Me too. Goodnight, Lucy.

Goodnight, John.

Setting her phone down, she snuggled underneath the covers, no longer sleepy as excitement vibrated through her body. Sucking in her lips, she stared at the picture in the dim moonlight filtering through her lacy curtain until her eyes grew heavy and sleep claimed her.

7

John's eyes grew larger as he neared the end of the lane and Lucy's little house came into view. *Work in progress?* Several shutters painted deep green were propped against the porch while several others were in various stages of sanding or repair. A large shed was to the side but there was no way to use it as a garage considering it listed slightly to one side and a heavy snow could bring it down. The front of the one-story house was painted white, but the side visible to him was faded and in serious need of attention.

He parked next to her little car, his large, new SUV dwarfing her older vehicle. He'd finally turned in his rental and purchased a similar SUV, spending more money than he thought possible for his wheels. But he had to admit, for his first big purchase since leaving the service, he chose well. Climbing down, he walked toward the front, uncertain if the porch would hold his weight.

The front door opened, and Lucy grinned up at him. "You found me! I'm so glad you're here!"

His delight at seeing her was thwarted slightly when he realized she was peering through a screen door that had no screen. She pushed on the door frame, opening it as she welcomed him inside.

"Good to be here. Thanks for inviting me." Once inside, he held her gaze, meeting her smile with one of his own.

"Make yourself at home. I need to check on the chicken." She waved her hand around the living space, adding, "I told you, it's a work in progress. I know it might seem a mess but I'm working on it slowly." Turning, she hurried down the short hall and disappeared into what he assumed was the kitchen.

He looked toward the living room, seeing rough, scarred wooden floors and a stone fireplace with built-in bookshelves on either side. The fireplace appeared sturdy although he had no idea what condition it was in. The bookshelves on either side were steadied with two-by-fours nestled among the books, keeping the bowed shelves from falling.

"You can come on back," she called, and he followed her voice, glancing inside the powder room to see a sink with the plumbing intact underneath but no faucets above. Shaking his head, he stopped just inside the kitchen. An old stove emitted delicious scents and he was grateful at least it worked properly. Her ass was perfectly displayed as she bent to take something from the refrigerator. Glad that appliance was working as well, he shifted his stance to hide the fact that blood was running from his brain to his cock.

"Do you need some help?"

She twisted around as she placed a large bowl on the counter and shook her head. "No, it's almost ready." She looked past him, a crinkle forming on her brow. "My table is rather small, so I think we'll serve our plates from here if that's okay."

He glanced behind him to see a small, round, wooden table that appeared to be antique with two chairs on either side. The chairs were also small, and he hoped they would support his weight. Looking back, he longed to smooth the worry from her face. "That's perfect. It's just us, and I'd rather it be easy and informal anyway."

With deft efficiency, she placed a pan of cheesy chicken enchiladas on a trivet sitting on the counter. Next, she placed bowls of guacamole, homemade salsa, sour cream, and cheese. Opening a large bag of tortilla chips, she poured them into another bowl.

"This looks great," he said, forgetting the state of her house and focusing on the food in front of him.

She thanked his compliment with a wide smile as she handed him a plate. "Go ahead and fill up, you can always come back for seconds and thirds if you want. What would you like to drink? I have iced tea, beer, wine..."

"Beer would be great."

She grabbed a couple of beers from the refrigerator and set them on the table. He continued to stand to the side, holding his plate, until she joined him. Once the dishes were piled high, he eased into the chair, making sure it would hold his weight despite its slight wobble. Her laughter greeted his ears, and he looked across the table.

"I can tell you're afraid to sit down, but honestly, that chair can hold my brother or my dad."

That told him her family must know the state of her house, and after a moment of eating, he dipped his toe into the questions. "So, it looks like you're doing some work around the place."

Her laughter rang out again, and he loved the sound of it.

"You're being very polite. And doing *some work around the place* would be an understatement, to hear my dad talk about it. He says my house is a disaster, and I'm a disaster in it!"

He frowned at the thought of her family not appreciating her efforts, but she quickly rushed to explain.

"He just worries, that's all. He and my brother come by sometimes to offer advice or to help, but they finally understand that I want to do most of it myself. Plus, they have jobs they need to take care of. My mom encourages my projects, but I think she worries a bit also. As long as I promised that I won't climb on the roof without letting one of them know, she's pretty chill about it all."

"I understand you doing the painting and tackling some of the carpentry, but I couldn't help but notice the plumbing in the bathroom…" He left the statement open-ended, hoping she wouldn't be offended.

Chewing, she swallowed first, then took a sip of beer

before hefting her shoulders in a shrug. "That's what YouTube videos are for."

His fork halted on the way to his mouth, his brow furrowing as he discerned her meaning. "You're watching YouTube videos to learn how to do the plumbing?"

She nodded with enthusiasm, her fork waving in the air as she spoke. "You can find YouTube videos on just about everything. I mean, I wouldn't try to do my electricity because I don't want to catch my house on fire or electrocute myself—"

"Thank God for that!"

Either she didn't hear his incredulity or chose to ignore him as she continued. "But I learned how to sand my shutters before painting them. I learned how to do a few repairs, although I find the plumbing a bit more difficult."

"Is there a reason you want to do it all yourself?"

He noticed a small dab of cheese on the corner of her mouth, and as her tongue darted out to lick it away, he wished he could have leaned across the table and done that for her. As she began to answer his question, he was forced to remind himself what he'd asked.

"Money, for one thing. I don't have the money to pay someone to do everything for this house that needs to be done. But the other thing is just setting a goal and wanting to see it through. I really like knowing that I'm putting my blood, sweat, and tears into this place."

"What will you do when you finish?"

She shrugged, her smile drooping slightly. "I'm not sure. I'm making it my own, but I don't know that it's my forever home. It's sort of hard to look into the future and know what I want." She glanced around. "I mean, it's a great cottage but too small for a family if I'm lucky enough to have one."

A flash of her being married slammed into his mind, and his breath caught in his throat, hating the idea of her with another man. *How the hell can I be jealous? We've just met.* But as soon as that thought hit him, he shook his head. *No, that's not true. We've been getting to know each other for the past eight months through the letters.*

"Are you okay?" she asked, drawing his gaze back to her. "You seemed lost in thought."

"Oh... I was just thinking of this place. Um... you seem to have several projects going on all at once."

A wide grin brightened her already-beautiful face. "I started on the shutters because that seemed easy. But then I hated the drip in the bathroom sink, so I decided to stop on the shutters and work on that first. Of course, that was all after I'd started to work on the shelves close to the fireplace. I think, as a homeowner, I'm very distractible when it comes to my projects."

His brows lifted. He wanted to offer to assist, but she'd already mentioned her family doing the same thing and she'd wanted to work on projects herself. *Still...* "Well, if you ever want someone to work with, just let me know. I've been doing projects on Gramps' house."

Her smile shot straight through his chest. Deciding to leave the subject of her house alone, he asked questions about her class, bringing an even brighter smile to her face. By the time they made it to double chocolate cake, he was more relaxed than he'd been in years.

Working side by side, they washed the dishes and put away the few leftovers. Grabbing two more beers, she led him on a tour of the house, excitedly detailing the improvements she wanted to make. It was hard not to catch her enthusiasm, and he chuckled at her many misadventure stories.

"I couldn't believe I didn't get stung when I found the hornet's nest behind the shutter on the side window. And don't even get me started on the attic. I know there's room for storage up there, but I poked my head up there and immediately shut the door! I'm terrified of bats! I found a snakeskin in the shed and that's why I haven't been back out there. My dad told me to stay out until he had a chance to check it out."

"Sounds like you're really close to your family."

They settled on the sofa, and she twisted her body so that she could face him with one leg tucked underneath her. Bright eyes sparkled as she talked about her cottage, her family, and her students. He loved hearing her voice, wanting to know everything about her, and fought the urge to reach over to take her hand or rest his fingers on her shoulder, anything to have a physical contact to match the emotional pull filling him.

She ducked her head and sighed. "I've talked so much that I've barely given you a chance to say anything."

"I like listening." Fascinated by her, he'd like to do more than listen. Staring at her lips that were so close, it would only take a short distance to be able to kiss her.

Holding back, he wanted to take it slow. *She's not like the women hanging around the base looking to score.* Blowing out a shallow breath, he hoped she would keep talking.

Her lips were still curved upward, but her eyes focused directly on his face. "I'd like to hear more about you. What you're doing, what your plans are."

Suddenly, the cold finger of self-consciousness moved over him, and he hesitated, lifting his hand to squeeze the back of his neck. "There's not much to tell that you don't already know. I joined the Army right after high school. Did sixteen years and flying shrapnel took away my career. So, right now, I'm out of a job, out of a career, living with my grandfather, and don't have a clue what's next."

As the words left his mouth, he hated the sound of the pity party they created. But Lucy was a beautiful, educated woman. Fully employed as a teacher. Surrounded by a family that cared for her, offering her advice and assistance when needed. And she was fixing up a house all on her own, just by learning, doing, making mistakes, and finding successes beyond those mistakes. *There's not a goddamn thing I've got to offer her. Right now, I'm an unemployed ex-soldier.*

Suddenly, the room seemed too small, the air too thick. He stood, placing his half-empty beer on the coffee table. "Listen, dinner was great but I'd better be going."

Her eyes widened as her mouth fell into a silent circle, her surprise evident. "O… kay…"

He walked to the door, his mind and body in agony as it battled the desire to offer her anything he could while knowing he had nothing to give. He was halfway down her porch steps by the time she had followed and reached out to grab his arm. He whirled around, hating the disappointment on her face.

"So... um... you'll still be at the school on Wednesday?"

His shoulders slumped, and he nodded. "Yeah... I'll be there."

"Okay, good. Well, I'll see you around? Maybe you can text... or something?"

He heard the hope in her voice but swallowed deeply, wanting to squash what he knew would lead to nothing. "I'll be pretty busy. Got lots to do for Gramps."

Her head nodded in jerks, and he hated the way her smile had turned tremulous. "Okay. Well... thanks for coming. Bye, John."

He offered a chin lift as he turned to walk out her door. *A fuckin' chin lift? Fine for the guys, but that sucks as a thank you for dinner.* He opened his mouth to refute his abrupt departure, lifting his hand toward her, but she had already backed through the door, her hand raised in a little wave. Turning, he stalked toward his SUV, climbing inside, a tidal wave of anger at himself threatening to sweep him away.

After a three-point turn, he drove down her long drive and allowed himself a last look in the rear-view mirror. She was standing at the window, staring out at him. His hand slammed against the steering wheel and he cursed the end of his career, the black that would always stay just to the left of him, being unemployed and feeling useless… and most of all, being a goddamn pussy for walking away from Lucy.

He had hoped his grandfather would already be in his room by the time he got home, but his luck wasn't holding out. As soon as he stepped into the house, Gramps, leaning back in his recliner, took one look at him and said, "What put that dark look on your face? Thought you were having dinner with that teacher?"

"Her name is Lucy."

"Okay, Lucy. But from the scowl on your face, I won't be meeting her anytime soon, so it doesn't matter what I call her. What happened? Her cooking bad?"

Scowling, he stomped over to the sofa and flopped down onto the cushions. "No, her cooking was fine."

Gramps muted the TV. "So, what's got your boxers in a twist?"

It was on the tip of his tongue to deny that his *boxers were in a twist*, but considering Gramps was reading him correctly, it would've been a foolish lie. Scrubbing his hand over his face, he leaned his head back and stared up at the ceiling. "She's great, the meal was fine, the conversation fun. But we're not right for each other, so it just didn't seem like there was any reason to stick around."

"Just not right for each other? What the hell does that mean? What's that word they use? High mainte-nance? Is that what she is? Or maybe she comes from a highfalutin family? Lives in a big house with a big bank account and thinks her shit don't stink?"

Bolting upright, John shook his head, the crinkle deepening in his forehead. "Gramps, she's none of that!

She's a hard-working teacher living in a cottage that seriously needs work, and she's convinced herself she can fix it up and make repairs, even though she's had to watch videos to discern the difference between a screwdriver and a hammer. And while her methods may be a little nuts, what she has accomplished looks good. She's beautiful in a very natural way. Comes from a working-class family that's close. And the dinner was good. Not fancy, but good eating and lots of it."

Gramps had a twinkle in his eyes when he leaned back in his recliner. "Hmph. I can certainly see why you came home in a bad mood after spending time with a woman like *that*." The silence closed in around them for a moment before Gramps finally asked, "Boy, you want to tell me what's really stuck in your craw?"

John continued to let the silence fill the room, but it settled like a scratchy wool blanket, one he wanted to toss off. "I've got no job, Gramps. For the past couple of weeks, I could pretend I was just on leave. Visiting here, helping you out, taking time off. But being with Lucy, knowing I'd like to see her again, it was like I was hit over the head with the realization that I'm an unemployed vet... an unemployed, limited vision vet."

The *whump* of the recliner snapping to an upright position sounded out in the room, and John jerked his head to the left so he'd have a clearer vision of his grandfather. His grandfather's scowl matched the expression etched onto his own face.

"Now that's a load of crap if I ever heard it. On top of that, you ought to be ashamed of yourself. I certainly am!"

Blinking, he opened his mouth but his grandfather's fist slamming down on the arm of his recliner stopped any words from coming.

"You got your health. Yeah, I know, you had an injury and lost part of your vision. But you can see. You can move. You came back with all your limbs. Looks to me like everything on you is working but your brain!" Gramps heaved a great sigh, his voice shaking. "Boy, I know you're not happy with how things played out, but a helluva lot more people came home in worse shape than you, and those are the ones who came home alive. Do you think I didn't worry? You think I didn't lay awake at night in fear of soldiers showing up at the door again like they did with your dad?"

Shame slithered through his body, threatening to choke off his breath. So focused on his disappointment, he'd never considered the emotions of his grandfather. "Fuck... I never thought..."

"That's what I'm saying. You aren't using your God-given brain other than feeling sorry for yourself."

Scrubbing his hand over his face, he let his head fall back onto the sofa cushion again. He thought of Kyle, whose broken ankle would probably never heal enough to allow him to go back as a SEAL. And Jaxson. He winced at the memory of Jaxson's injuries. *I need to text those guys. Check up on them. Do something besides just bemoaning my situation.* "You're right, Gramps." His voice was soft, his words resigned.

"Getting injured just four years out of retirement sucks, John. I get that. But you've got possibilities out there. Hell, Horace is setting you up with a meeting with his boss. And if that don't work out, there are other things for you. So, maybe the time isn't right for you and this teacher—Lucy. But that don't mean you don't have a helluva lot to offer the right woman."

Before John had a chance to respond, Gramps pushed himself out of the recliner and mumbled, "Going to bed. I've said my piece, and you can chew it over." He walked stiffly up the stairs, his hand tossed upward in the air as his silent *'goodnight'*.

John sat alone in the dark living room for a long time, memories of the past vying for attention with thoughts of the present. But when he finally headed to bed, it was the disappointed expression in Lucy's eyes as he abruptly left her house that followed him into sleep.

8

Lucy sat alone in her classroom, opening the plastic bag with her sandwich and chips. She usually ate in the teacher's lounge but today wasn't in the mood for the lively chats. Not when her mind was still filled with the infuriating John Roster.

She had tried to hide her rotten mood during her family dinner yesterday, but they knew something was up. Thankfully, her parents hadn't continued to pry, having always allowed her to noodle through her problems... well, after her dad made sure her house wasn't falling apart. Her brother wanted to know if he needed to kick some guy's ass, but she assured him she was perfectly capable of kicking ass if needed. Her mother had offered a little smile, instinctively knowing she was upset over a man.

But the truth was she had no idea why John had turned cold on her. They'd had a nice dinner. They'd talked about house projects and her class. He'd seemed relaxed. Sitting on the sofa, she had imagined that they were leaning toward each other as they talked, his fingers dancing close to her shoulder. She had even considered closing the distance and seeing if he tasted as good as she was sure he would. And from the look in his eyes, he'd wanted that, too. *So what happened? I ask more about him and suddenly he clams up and can't get out of my house fast enough.*

A knock on the door had her look up and she smiled as Paula walked in, glad for the distraction.

"Hey, girl, my kids are at art class so I thought I'd have a little adult time while yours are at lunch." Paula plopped down into the chair next to Lucy's desk and narrowed her eyes. "You certainly don't look like a woman who had dinner with a delicious soldier over the weekend."

She shrugged. "It was nice but other than him coming on Wednesday to visit my classroom again, I'm not sure I'll see him. I don't think he's that into me."

"Oh, Lucy, I'm sorry. I thought for sure he was interested when you were together at Moose's the other night. He certainly looked like he would slay a dragon for you."

A snort slipped out, and she shook her head. "Dinner was nice, and we chatted easily. At least, I did. But when I asked more about him, he suddenly took off like I'd asked him to divulge government secrets or something. I guess he was just being polite and then decided that he wasn't interested." She shrugged again. "Oh, well. I can see him on Wednesday when he comes here, be congenial, and then it will be over. Since he's out of the Army, there won't be any more class assignments that involve him anyway."

"Well, since you're still a free agent, I've got a proposal. There's a music festival in Canada this weekend and I've got two tickets for the VIP section, including free beer. You and me, girl. Music. Beer. Special passes to meet the band. What do you say?"

"Are you going for the band or your new friends in the biker jackets?"

Paula jerked her chin back, her eyes narrowing. "Seriously, Lucy? When did you start having a prejudice against bikers?"

"I don't," she huffed, tossing her balled-up napkin onto the table. "I have no problem with someone's appearance or what they like to do, including riding, as long as what they do isn't illegal."

"Are you saying those guys I was with Friday night are criminals? Based on what? Their looks? Their jackets?"

Licking her lips, she said, "No, but John didn't have a good feeling about them."

Paula threw her hands into the air. "Well, oh, my God. Soldier-boy John didn't have a good feeling about them. Well, let me just go hide under a rock before the big, bad bikers come to get me!"

"You don't have to get all sarcastic. That's not help-ing." They sat in silence, Lucy enduring Paula's glare for a moment, before she finally said, "I don't want us to argue."

Paula sighed heavily and nodded. "I don't either. Look, this weekend has nothing to do with the bikers anyway. I just got angry when you asked about them. But this weekend is about the music festival." She reached over and squeezed Lucy's hand. "And John didn't turn out to be the great hero you had in your mind, so I'm not sure why his opinion matters anyway. Come on. Say you'll go with me."

It was on the tip of her tongue to say no, but the idea of being home alone for another weekend just working on her house held little appeal. Sucking in a deep breath before letting it out in a rush, she looked up at Paula's expectant face. "Okay."

Paula jerked slightly. "What? Just like that? Okay? No *'I've got to paint my ceiling'* excuse?"

Rolling her eyes, she crinkled her nose. "I don't always have excuses!"

"Once you bought your house, you turned into a little old lady. But I'm just teasing. I'm stoked about this weekend. I'll pick you up on Saturday morning and we'll make a day of it." Paula stood and smoothed her skirt before walking to the door. She turned and winked. "And if we get lucky, we'll spend the night there, too!"

Paula left the room before Lucy had a chance to retort. Sighing heavily, she packed up her half-eaten sandwich and placed it back into her bag, needing to run to the restroom before her class came back into the room. She wished she had more enthusiasm for Paula's weekend adventure. They'd certainly had fun before when they went to concerts or movies together, but it seemed Paula's tastes had recently turned a little wilder. *Or maybe I'm just becoming an old lady like she said.*

John was at the top of the ladder, repairing some of Gramps' guttering that had pulled loose from the edge of the roof. With only a few small trees in the vicinity of the house, at least he didn't have to clean out the gutters first. An image of Lucy's cottage in the woods with tall trees all around caused him to wonder about the condition of her gutters. He remembered she'd said her mother didn't want her to climb onto the roof, but she didn't mention whether or not she'd been on a ladder.

He hated the way he left things with her, and the desire to call or at least send a text just to know that she was okay was strong. Maybe to tell her he was sorry. Maybe to tell her they could start over.

He'd taken his grandfather's words to heart the other evening but couldn't brush away the feeling that he had nothing to offer her at the moment. *Well, I can always offer to help her with her gutters, but I doubt that would go over very well.*

He was lost in thought, but years in special forces had honed his senses to a fine point and he heard a vehicle slow down before it turned onto Gramps' drive. Twisting around, he watched as a large, black SUV drove to the house, parking next to Gramps' old truck. Horace climbed down from the passenger side, throwing his hand up in a wave toward Gramps, who had stepped out onto the front porch.

The driver of the vehicle alighted, and John had no doubt he was looking at Horace's boss, the owner of Lighthouse Security Investigations. The man was tall and broad, with black hair and a shadowed jaw. His eyes were covered by aviator glasses, and he walked with an air of confidence and accomplishment. Horace was in the process of introducing Gramps but he was aware the man's gaze shot up the ladder toward him.

Climbing down, nervousness bolted through him, an emotion he wasn't used to. But considering he'd felt the same thing before going into the school last week, he wondered if being outside his comfort zone was something he would have to get used to. Not liking that thought, he shoved it to the side as he reached the bottom of the ladder. Pulling off his leather work gloves, he dropped them, along with a hammer, to the ground and stepped forward.

Gramps was grinning ear to ear, a sight he'd rarely seen. "John, you remember my friend, Horace."

Reaching out his hand, he shook the older man's firm grip. "Good to see you again."

Horace nodded, smiling. "Good to see you, too. As I promised, I talked to my boss. I'd like you to meet Mason Hanover. Mace, this is John Roster."

The two men shook hands, outwardly friendly but both sizing each other up and knowing that was exactly what they were doing.

"John," Mace began. "Horace suggested spending some time with your grandfather, so I thought I'd come along and we could have a chance to meet and talk informally."

"I'd like that, sir."

"It's just Mace, not sir."

Gramps piped up. "Why don't you go sit inside the

house? There's beer or iced tea, and Horace is going to take me into town to pick up a couple of things. We'll take my truck so if Mace needs to leave, he can do so, and I can drop Horace off at his place."

John left the decision up to Mace but wasn't surprised at the other man's easy acquiescence. Soon, the two older men left, and he and Mace were in the living room, beers in front of them.

"Why don't you tell me a bit about yourself, John?"

Mace's demeanor was casual, but John knew the man was sharp and intuitive, anything but casual. This was the initial stage of a job interview, and he was certain Mace would pick up on every nuance. *All I can be is me. Either he thinks I've got possibilities or I don't, but his opinion has to be based on the real me.* The tension he'd carried in his shoulders eased with that thought, and he leaned forward, resting his forearms on his knees as he held Mace's gaze.

"My pre-military background was varied. My father was in the Army, and my early years were spent moving around a lot. My parents got a divorce when I was about ten, and my dad had custody. When he was deployed, I would come here and stay with my grandparents. When I was thirteen, my dad was killed in an accident during a training maneuver and I moved here permanently with my grandparents. I was lucky to have them in my life. But like many, I was anxious to chart my own way and joined the Army right out of high school. After a couple of years, I was accepted into Special Forces Preparation Course."

Mace's lips curved slightly, and John grinned. "It's

my understanding that you were Special Forces, so I'm sure you know this part of my story. SF Assessment and Selection and SFQC. After the year of Qualification Course, I graduated and became the Eighteen C."

Mace nodded. "Build it, demolish it."

"Yes, sir—Mace. I was lucky. Had a career I loved and was SF for twelve of my sixteen years."

"I won't ask you about duties or missions, well acquainted with all of those. But I am curious about your discharge."

"It was the last mission I was on. I'd managed the demolition with no problem, but one of my team members was injured, and I went to help. An IED exploded near us, and I took a hit on the left side of my face with shrapnel. Honestly, it wasn't that bad, but it was the placement of the injury. I had a few pieces in my eye." He lifted his hand, his fingers touching the already-familiar scars. "I was temporarily blinded but was helicoptered out and lucky to have an ophthalmo-logic surgeon to save my sight." He shrugged, but sat up straight, holding Mace's gaze. "But I have no peripheral vision in my left eye on that side." He lifted his hand in front of him and slowly moved it toward the left, stop-ping at a seventy-five-degree angle from his face. "I can see to here, and from then on to my shoulder is black."

Mace held his gaze, saying nothing for a moment, then nodded slowly. "You would be a liability to your SF team without your full vision."

Mace's words were completely true. John knew it. He understood it. That liability was the entire reason he was no longer able to serve on his SF team. It would be the reason for him to have only a desk job if he'd stayed in the Army. His mouth felt dry, and he swallowed with difficulty. He refused to look away from Mace's close perusal, knowing that the man's next words were probably going to tell him that his vision would be a liability in any security business and would therefore keep him from being employable with Lighthouse Security. But if that was what was going to come, he'd take it and not flinch. He'd just have to find another career. *This is not going to fuckin' define me.*

As though Mace heard his thoughts, he asked, "What defines you?"

He breathed deeply, considering his response. "De Oppresso Liber."

Mace's lips curved. "To free the oppressed."

"You might think I'm full of shit and feeding you a line. But for many years, the motto of the Special Forces defined me. For a couple of months, I admit I let my vision and subsequent medical discharge keep me from feeling the same sense of purpose. But the truth of the matter, Mace, is that I'm a protector at heart."

Mace leaned back in his seat, the beer bottle dangling loosely from his fingertips, and nodded. Tension eased out of John's body, knowing whatever Mace's decision would be, he'd been truthful.

"My background is classified, but I can say that I struggled with a change I had to make mid-mission but knew the position I'd taken would save lives. It was on this special operation that I had the opportunity to work with a multi-agency task force of SEALs, Rangers, Deltas, Air Force Special Ops, and CIA, plus some others. I couldn't imagine how it was going to work but discovered when egos were checked at the door, the talents and special knowledge from this diverse group of people meant that we accomplished a great deal. It became a dream of mine that when I left the Army I could replicate the idea for a private security business. It took five years, calling in markers for many of my contacts, and a lot of money to create Lighthouse Security Investigations. We run private and government contracts. We pick and choose the missions we feel are best suited for our specialties. I consider my Keepers to be the best in the business."

He nodded, interest flaring but uncertain if he should ask any questions. Knowing Mace would not divulge any specifics on their cases, he waited to see what other information would be imparted.

"My situation was similar to yours, only it was my dad that had taken off and my mom raised my sister and me. I spent a lot of time with my grandfather who lived near a lighthouse not too far from here. I grew up listening to the stories of the lighthouse keepers, their sense of dedication and devotion to the task regardless of the conditions they were forced to live in. Keepers are the defenders of the light. The caretakers. The guides to safety for those who are lost in the storm."

"I'm impressed, Mace. Not only with the business you built but with your vision for the mission you undertake."

"Thank you, I appreciate that. I don't advertise for employees. And I assure you that just because someone was in a branch of special operations in the military, that doesn't give them an automatic *in* with me. Our employee base is fairly small, and I'm not looking to expand beyond our capabilities. I started with nine Special Ops, and a former CIA Special Ops I'd worked with is running the office. That position was her choice, even though now she also works some ops with us. I'd worked with Horace's wife, and when they'd both retired years before and were looking for something to do, I hired them on as well. He takes care of the grounds, and quite frankly, Marge takes care of us. I've now increased our ranks by four more. My wife is also now our office manager."

John tried to tamp down his growing enthusiasm but was certain that Mace would not be divulging this much information if he wasn't at least interested in considering him as a possible employee.

They continued to talk for another hour, both about missions they were able to discuss and getting to know each other more. Just as Gramps returned home, they stood and walked out to Mace's SUV.

Shaking hands, Mace said, "I'd like for you to have a chance to meet some of the other Keepers."

"I'd like that. I'd like that a great deal."

"Okay, how about Thursday night at Moose's Bar? It's a local establishment."

"I've been there. That's where I met Horace."

"Good, good. Thursday nights tend to be less crowded and a lot tamer than the weekends. We'll get there about seven."

"I'll be there."

Mace climbed into his SUV, and John threw his

hand up in a wave as he watched it drive back down Gramps' drive before he headed inside. Gramps looked up at him, his eyes sharp.

"Good visit, boy?"

"Yeah, Gramps. Good visit."

Gramps nodded and settled into his recliner. "Well, don't forget the gutters."

Walking back outside, he grinned as he climbed the ladder once again.

9

Wednesday dawned dreary, a chilly Maine spring with rain in the forecast. As the children talked excitedly about John's visit, Lucy had to pull from deep within her optimistic reserves to not want to cancel the entire visit. *I can do this. I can be professional. I can be pleasant. Just a visit from someone the children corresponded with. Not my crush. Not my dream man. Not my... anything.*

Huffing, she flipped the light switch a few times to bring the children to order and had them take their seats again just as the rain pelted against the windows. Giving them their last instructions while Mrs. Farthingale had gone to fetch John from the office, she heard footsteps approach. Steeling her spine, she plastered a wide smile on her face and turned to face the door. But seeing him enter, his gaze sweeping over the classroom and not stopping until landing on her, her breath left her lungs in a rush. She was saved from embarrassment only because the children clapped to welcome him.

Walking forward with her hand outstretched, she

ignored the flash of doubt she noted in his eyes and greeted, "Welcome back, Sergeant Roster."

His eyes widened slightly but that was the only way she could determine that indicated he might have wondered how she would greet him. He took her hand in his, and she hoped he didn't feel the tremble in her fingers. His gaze shot down to her hand. *I should have known the super-soldier would notice that!*

"It's nice to see you again, Ms. Carrington."

His rich, low voice was like velvet, and she sucked in another breath to steady herself. "As you can see, the class is excited to have you come for an official visit. We'll start with some questions, if you don't mind, giving you plenty of time to talk, and then a few of our parents have sent in goodies."

"Whatever you have planned will be fine with me," he said, holding her gaze before smiling toward the class.

Leaning closer, she lowered her voice. "If we start with the snacks, the sugar rush will create havoc. This way, they can get on the bus and get home before they start bouncing off the walls."

His smile widened, threatening to melt her resolve to keep their contact professional. Clearing her throat, she led him to a tall chair in front of the class.

"Thank you, but I prefer to stand if you don't mind." He waved toward the chair and added, "Please, Ms. Carrington. I'd be honored if you'd sit."

"Oh... sure." She approached the chair and startled as his hand encircled her arm as she hefted up into the seat. "Thanks," she said, wishing the feel of his hand on her didn't make her heart race. Now facing the class with him standing next to her, she called on the first student to ask their question.

"Why did you join the military?"

He nodded at the solemn-faced boy. "Well, my father had been in the Army. I got to live in lots of different places when he was able to take me with him. I liked seeing new places and meeting new people. I always thought of him as a hero, and I wanted to be like him."

"What kind of food did you have to eat?" That question came from a little girl, her cheeks puffed from her wide smile as she stared up at him, her eyes beaming.

"When I was in the United States, my food was just like yours. We had a cafeteria or could cook our own food, or we ate out. But when we were overseas, sometimes in really remote areas, we had to take our food with us or eat what we could find." He hesitated, casting a glance toward Lucy. "It was sometimes a bit strange... like, I've eaten snakes and sometimes bugs."

The class erupted in groans mixed with laughter. Lucy lifted her fingers to her lips, unable to hide her smile. Casting her gaze up at him, she nodded for him to continue.

"I suppose the most important thing we had to do was to make sure our water was safe to drink. You can go a lot longer without food than you can water. So, we had ways to make it potable... drinkable if it was... um... not clean."

"What did you do in the Army?"

"I was the Engineer Sergeant of a special team of soldiers. I had to be accepted into the training program and then there were almost two years of training. I made it through, and my job was to be able to build things, like bridges and buildings. I was also trained to be able to demolish things, which means I got to safely... uh... knock things down when necessary." His brow furrowed as he shot another look at Lucy.

She offered a little nod to indicate she appreciated him making sure his comments were appropriate for ten-year-olds, even if most of them had played video games that included pretend explosions and more things than she wished they'd been exposed to.

One of her quietest girls in the class raised her hand. "What were the best things about being in the Army and what do you miss the most?"

He sighed lightly and nodded, appearing to give great consideration to her question. "I suppose it was the friendships. My teammates. We got up every day and knew what needed to be done and we accomplished it together. We felt pride in what we did. We cooperated at all times. If we didn't, one of us might get injured or worse. But we really cared about each other. When one of us succeeded, we all succeeded. And I miss that now that I'm out."

The kids peppered him with a few more questions, but Lucy tuned them out, his last words resonating deep inside. His loneliness. His lack of friends. His lack of purpose. *I asked him to talk about himself, but he wasn't ready.* That reality slammed into her and a gasp slipped from her lips.

He jerked his head to the side to look at her, but she

plastered another smile on her face, ignoring the unspoken question in his furrowed brow.

Turning back to the class, he continued. "I do have to say that sometimes, even with teammates, it can be lonely, and the letters you sent as well as the goodie packages made my service time this past year a lot better."

He looked back at her and she smiled again, this time less forced. "Okay, class, that's enough questions for now. How about we offer Sergeant Roster some food to commemorate his being back home?"

The children lined up at the back table where Mrs. Farthingale had placed several platters of brownies, chips, and cookies. They waited while she invited John to go first and then he delighted her when he sat with the kids at their tables, answering more questions and making the kids feel important.

"He's something else, isn't he?" Mrs. Farthingale asked as she and Lucy stood at the table munching.

Nodding slowly as John spoke gently to one of her students who was shy. "Yes, he is."

"Do I detect a little spark there?"

A rueful snort escaped. "I think he needs more time to discover who he is outside of the Army first."

"I think that's a very wise intuition." Mrs. Farthingale nodded, patting her arm.

Lucy remained quiet but could have easily refuted that it was not her intuition. *More like a hard-learned lesson.*

The bell soon rang, and the kids headed out the door with the aide, leaving Lucy alone with John. She had no idea what to expect, thinking he might hurry out with them, but instead, he remained behind, uncertainty in his eyes.

Approaching, she smiled. "Thank you so much for coming. They enjoyed hearing your stories."

"It was my pleasure. It was easier this time. Last week I was nervous about coming here. But I wanted to make sure they knew that I appreciated their bringing a bit of home to me when I was serving." He hesitated, casting his eyes downward before lifting them to hold her gaze. "I know the class project was your idea, so I need to let you know I'm grateful as well."

"It was good for all of us, too." A flash of his photograph on her nightstand flew through her mind, but she simply smiled, her hands clasped in front of her.

"Listen, Lucy, I need to apologize for the way I left your house—"

"No, you don't. It was fine. I'm sure you were very tired and… um… it was fine." His lips pressed tightly together, and she hated the look of doubt in his eyes. Sighing, she placed her hand on his arm, wanting nothing but honesty between them. "John, I'm sure that being back home has created a mixed bag of emotions. You get to be with your grandfather again but listening to you today made me realize that you had to say goodbye to many of your friends, and I know that was hard. You're going through a lot of changes right now, and… Well, if you ever need a home-cooked meal, you've got my number."

Relief flooded his face, and he nodded. "I have a line on a possible job. I met with the owner of the business, and I'll have the opportunity to meet some of the other people on his staff tomorrow. I don't know if anything will come from it, but... Well, I just wanted you to know."

With her hand still on his arm, she squeezed gently, smiling. "That's wonderful. I hope it's something that you'd like to do and it turns out in a positive way." His lips curved slightly, and even a little smile from him made her day brighter.

"So, do you have any home projects this weekend you're going to work on?"

Chuckling, she said, "While there's always a project ready to be worked on, I'm going to go to a concert in Canada with my friend Paula this weekend. We'll leave on Saturday morning and get back very late Saturday evening."

His brow lowered and he opened his mouth to speak, then snapped it shut. She waited to see what he wanted to say but had a feeling she knew where his thoughts had gone. "I know she didn't make a good impression on you the other day, but it's just a music concert in Sherbrooke. Only about a four-hour drive. We've gone to these before, and it will be fine. To be honest, I asked her about the biker she was with. While I wasn't crazy about her answer, she admitted that this trip was for the music only."

For the next several minutes, he helped her straighten the room, getting it prepared for the next day. She grabbed her purse and her school bag, and he walked her to the teachers' parking lot. Standing at her car, she looked up, fighting the urge to smooth the worried crinkle in his forehead.

"Lucy, I know I don't have any right to ask this, but if you need anything, please, give me a call. Anything at all."

"Thank you. I'll be fine, but thank you." She climbed into her car, her eyes continually moving to her rearview mirror as she pulled away. The sight of him growing smaller in the mirror tugged at her heartstrings. *Maybe friendship is all we'll ever have, but I'll take it. Somehow, I think being friends with John would be better than not having him in my life at all.* With another sigh, she turned the corner as she headed home, his image no longer in sight.

John walked into Moose's Bar again, only this time the nerves snaking through him were tinged with eager excitement. His eyes adjusted to the dark interior quickly, and he spotted Mace sitting with a large group at two tables pushed together. A grin stretched his lips as he shot his gaze over the others. Fit, muscular bodies. Sharp, intelligent eyes that were clocking him as soon as he entered. Even if he hadn't been told they were Special Ops, it was evident to him that they were more than your average soldiers. For an instant, it was like walking into a bar near the base in North Carolina where his team was stationed between missions.

Mace stood as he approached, his hand out in greeting. "John, good to see you, again."

"Mace, thanks for inviting me here."

Mace turned to the others sitting at the table. "I've got a few of my friends here for you to meet as well. Starting to my left are Walker, Drew, Babs, and Rank. Across the table are Tate, Cobb, Blake, Josh, and Bray."

At the last introduction, he did a double-take, his eyes widening in recognition at the man grinning up at him. "Allan Bray? Holy shit, man." Bray laughed as he stood up, wrapping him in a bear hug, both men slapping each other on the back.

Separating, he glanced over to see the others grinning and Mace's eyes pinned on the two men. "Bray and I never served on the same team, but we ran a few joint missions. If shit went down, he was a well-known medic."

Bray laughed, offering a shrug toward Mace. "I didn't recognize the name John Roster when you mentioned it. I just knew him as Wrecker. Best demolition sergeant."

After that surprise, John settled next to Mace and ordered a beer. Bray looked over, his smile still firmly in place before turning to the other Keepers. "This guy destroyed a fuckin' munitions compound on a mission. Did it faster than anyone on either team thought possible. The rest of his team had to hustle to get the recovery out of there. My team's eighteen-C was one of the best, but he was fuckin' green with envy over that job you completed."

Tension eased as John relaxed, thrilled that with that one endorsement from Bray the others smiled, their gazes less assessing than he'd recognized when he walked in.

The conversation amongst the gathering was light considering they were in public, focusing mostly on their military careers. To an observer, it would appear as members of the local American Legion having a few beers after a meeting. It was easy to spot the teasing, competitive camaraderie between the former Navy SEALs and the Army Rangers, Deltas, and Special Forces. He discovered that Drew was their pilot and Bray continued to function as a medic. After an hour, he was completely at ease and impressed as hell with what Mace had brought together for his business.

As Mace signaled to the server for another round, he shifted toward John. "If you're interested, I'd like to offer you a chance to come to visit our headquarters. There would be an NDA for you to sign, and if we come to an agreement after that, a probationary employment status would take effect."

He forced his breathing to remain steady, glancing down the table to see the smiles on the others' faces before turning back to the boss. "Mace, I don't have to think about it more than what I already have. I'm honored to have this opportunity."

Mace's stone expression cracked slightly as his lips curved upward. He held out his hand and the two men clasped palms together. "I'll have Sylvie, my wife as well as our office manager, call you with the details."

The server brought more pitchers, and the conversations once again became easy. The crowd in Moose's Bar was small, making it easy to observe the other patrons, all seeming to know Mace, occasionally tossing up a hand or chin lift in greeting. The comfortable vibe made it evident that when the door opened and a few bikers walked and headed to the back, the group he was with stiffened, their eyes sharp once again. John spied the same insignia on their patches as the ones that had been there the other night—the same ones Paula had been hanging with.

Tuning in to the others' reactions, he looked to Mace. "What do you know about them?"

Mace's granite expression gave no emotion other than the glitter in his eyes. "Idle curiosity?"

"Not at all. A… friend was in here the other night with someone who was hanging around guys with the same patches. Gave me a bad feeling. Lucy wants nothing to do with them, but I'm not sure about her friend."

"Lucy?" Babs asked, her brow quirked upward.

He glanced down at the table. "Lucy Carrington. Local teacher. Her class project was me." Seeing the questioning stares peering at him, he shook his head. "They wrote to a local soldier. I was the lucky bastard who got a piece of home sent to him each month. Met the teacher and the class when I got back." Turning back to Mace, he said, "She's solid, but I've got a bad feeling about her friend who was cozying up to one of them."

"Minotaurs."

The one word growled from Mace had no meaning to John so he remained silent, waiting for more.

"Outlaw biker gang, mostly in Canada. Work with Hell's Angels here as part of their pipeline. Run drugs, guns, women, and if our intel is correct, possibly more." He leaned closer, his voice cold with conviction. "You tell Lucy to stay the hell away from them at all costs. Her friend doesn't follow suit? Then Lucy should not engage, not challenge. She *disengages*, even from the friendship."

"Fuck," John cursed as he exhaled heavily. "Lucy and this friend are going to Sherbrooke in Quebec this weekend to a music concert. Her friend has already promised that it's music only and nothing to do with the bikers."

"Fuck. Minotaurs and Hell's Angels' territory," Clay murmured. "Dealt with them before."

The cold fingers of fear for her threatened to overtake the good time he was having, and he pulled out his phone, tapping out a text.

Worried about you. Paula's new friends are trouble. Take care and remember to call me if you have any problems.

He sighed and shoved his phone back into his pocket, uncertain when she would get the message or how she'd react. He'd stupidly walked away from her, forcing them into the friend-only zone. *At least, I hope we're friends.* He wasn't sure about that status, but it seemed after his visit yesterday to her class, she'd warmed up to him again. He reached up and squeezed the back of his neck, swallowing his grimace so as not to draw attention to himself.

The gathering soon broke up, the others taking off in their vehicles after he shook their hands, accepting their enthusiasm for his visit to the Lighthouse headquarters. When it was just him, Bray, and Mace left in the parking lot, he turned to the iconic leader of the Keepers. "Mace, I can't thank you enough for the opportunity."

"I'm a good judge of character, John, but have to admit that you having Bray's commendation goes a long way as well. I'll have my Sylvie get in touch and send the paperwork you'll need to complete before a meeting on our turf." With a final wave, Mace turned and climbed into his large SUV.

He looked at Bray and shook his hand. "Thanks, man. This means the world to me."

"It's you, Wrecker. Mace won't take just anyone who served in Special Operations. Just being a former military elite isn't nearly enough to make a Keeper. But you impressed him, and what I know of you, you'll be an asset." Bray chuckled, clapping John on the shoulder. "Hell, man, I'm thrilled. It'll be great to finally work on the same team with you."

With final handshakes, he walked toward his SUV, glancing to the side at the bikes parked nearby. *Minotaurs. Drugs. Guns. Women. And Paula's got Lucy on their radar. Fuckin' hell.*

For the drive to Gramps', he thought of how to convince Lucy that she was better off not going on her trip but came up empty. Parking outside, he smiled as Gramps waved from the porch. Walking toward him, Gramps grinned.

"You look like it went well, boy."

Nodding, he opened the front door, allowing his grandfather to enter before him. "It did. Turns out I knew one of the men who works for Mace. We'd met in the service."

Gramps turned a sharp eye to him. "Good. Always helps to have someone on the inside to put in a good word."

"You hungry, Gramps?" he asked as they walked into the kitchen. "I can rustle up some chops."

"Wouldn't turn 'em down if they came at me."

Grinning, he moved about the small kitchen, starting to work on dinner.

"So... you gettin' the job?" Gramps pressed, settling into a kitchen chair.

"Probationary status. Got some forms to fill out, and I'll make a trip there to check out their headquarters, see what they do, and make sure it'll be a fit for me."

"Hmph."

"Don't worry. It'll be a fit." Placing the chops into the cast iron frying pan, he twisted around to look over his shoulder. "You know, it's kind of weird, but I met a fellow serviceman at the airport when I was coming here. He talked to me about the security business. I'd just never made a backup plan, so I hadn't given it any thought. But," he shrugged and turned back to the stove, "it feels right"

"Sometimes that's all we can go on, boy. Make a decision based on what our brain tells us makes sense and our gut tells us is right."

An image of Lucy flashed through his mind. He'd spent eight months thinking she was an older, grandmotherly woman, just getting to know her as a caring person and teacher. Meeting her in person put his admiration squarely in sync with his overwhelming, newfound attraction to her. *My gut told me she was right. Why the hell didn't I listen to it instead of my insecurities?*

By the time he climbed into bed, his excitement over his new career path with Lighthouse Security was overshadowed by thoughts of Lucy. He wished he had a do-over of their date a week ago. A chance to tell her he was getting a job. He had a future. How life had changed so quickly, and unlike when he was injured, this time it was for the better.

He tried to read for an hour, but after turning the pages realized he hadn't actually read the words. Finally, his phone vibrated and he grabbed it off the nightstand. Dropping his chin, he read the message.

Thanks for the heads up. I'll be fine. Just going for the music. Have a nice weekend.

While her message wasn't dismissive, it sure as fuck wasn't encouraging, either.

"I can't believe how she runs the grade-level meetings," Paula laughed. "I have a better time communicating with my third-graders! I honestly thought about talking to the principal but we're so close to the end of the year and Bonnie's term as grade-level chair is up, so I'll just suck it up and deal."

"I'm lucky. Cindy is great. In fact, she's so good, she's been our leader for three years." Lucy opened a soda, handing it to Paula before opening another one for herself.

"Oh, I love this song!" Paula turned the radio up, bouncing in her seat in time to the music.

Lucy laughed, loving the lighthearted atmosphere of their drive. They traveled on roads through thick forests once they left Portland heading north. The spring morning was cool, the trees were green, and the sky peeking through the forest overhead was bright blue. As always, she was reminded how much she loved Maine. Other people talked about the sun and fun of the east coast beaches, the great canyons of the west, and the charm of the south, but being born and raised in Maine, she didn't mind visiting other places but loved her gorgeous northern state.

The trip reminded her of others she and Paula had taken in the last couple of years. Their conversation was easy, sprinkled with laughter, gossip, and listening to music.

"I can't believe I snagged tickets for this music festival. There are two headliner bands, about six or seven smaller ones, and I've already checked out the venue in the park. Once we get our hands stamped going through the gates, we can move about freely. Food trucks, shop vendors, everything. And we have VIP passes for great seats just to the side of the stage."

"How on earth did you score those?"

Paula laughed as she looked over and winked. "It helps to know people in the right places."

"So that's what you call it when you get cozy with some of the band members?"

"You know it, girl!"

After several hours, they reached the border crossing into Canada between Canaan and Hereford. Paula slowed to a stop, and Lucy was glad traffic was not heavy. It only took a few minutes and they made it to the customs agents, answering a few questions. Lucy watched as one of the agents with his dog on a leash walked slowly around their car before they were waved to move on.

"I know it's probably irrational, but I always get nervous when I see the drug dogs. It doesn't matter that

I have nothing, we have nothing... there's that fear the dog will suddenly start barking."

Paula glanced to the side and nodded. "Well, I'm sure the drug runners know how to get drugs across the border without stuffing them right in the car that goes under the nose of an agent."

Lucy blinked, twisting her head to the side to stare at her friend. "Wow, Paula, that in no way makes me feel better!"

A bark of laughter came from Paula as she shrugged. "I'm just saying I think the serious smugglers know how to get around these borders."

Soon, they entered Sherbrooke, and Paula drove carefully through the streets as they made their way with GPS to the downtown area, getting them as close to the Jacques-Cartier Park as possible. But they were not the only festival goers with this idea, and she had to park almost six blocks away.

"It's okay," Lucy assured. "After being in the car for several hours, I need to walk anyway."

"I'm only thinking about when the concert is over and we've been drinking. I have a feeling tonight I'll hate having to get all the way to the car!"

Lucy hopped from the vehicle, ready to be out of Paula's small car, and turned to grab her bag. She had traded her purse for a small backpack and double-checked to make sure she had her wallet and phone. "Come on, let's go. I'm starving."

Paula grabbed her bag and nodded. "You're right. Let's get inside, find the VIP spot, and then hit the food trucks!"

The two wandered down the sidewalk of the city, soon coming to the park. Grass, trees, and a pond all combined to give the festival site a beautiful venue. The signs were in French, but since Paula was bilingual and Lucy knew enough French to get by, they had no problem finding their way around.

On their way to the VIP section, the scents emitting from the food trucks had Lucy's mouth watering. "I've got to stop now. Anyway, the lines aren't long." She headed to a vendor selling crepes, deciding on savory ones while Paula bought fish and chips. They got enough for both of them before walking to the beer vendors. Once their arms were full, they sat on the grass and divided the food between them. The sun was shining, the sound of children laughing filled the air, and one of the bands in the distance provided the perfect backdrop.

While Paula kept up a running monologue about the bands, Lucy, with her belly now full, allowed her mind to wander—and it didn't have to wander far to land on John. A little smile graced her face as she thought of being here with him and wondered what kind of music he liked. She wondered how his job interview went. And she worried. Even if he hadn't bounced between hot and cold with her, she couldn't turn off her emotions so quickly.

"Earth to Lucy."

She jumped, jerking her head to see Paula laughing.

"Your mind was a million miles away, and I have a feeling it had to do with the elusive soldier."

"I was just letting the sun soak into me, thinking

what a perfect day this is." There was a time when she was more certain of her friendship with Paula that she would have been truthful, but now the lie fell easily from her tongue, not wanting to share her thoughts of John. She sucked in her lips as she watched Paula lean back with her hands planted on the ground behind her. When a man walked by and glanced her way, she shook her long, blonde hair over her shoulders and arched slightly, making her breasts push upward, then laughed when the man's gaze dropped to her chest. *Has she always been so desperate for male attention?* Professionally paired together a couple of years ago, they'd started hanging together. *But is it a true friendship or am I just someone Paula hangs out with because she doesn't make girl-friends easily?* Deciding the day was too beautiful for such deep questions, she turned her attention back to the delicious food.

After they finished eating and tossed their trash, they walked to the VIP seats to the side of the stage. Obtaining passes, they grabbed seats and settled in, enjoying the band that was playing. An hour later, it was time for one of the headliner bands, and as they took the stage, Paula was dancing in the aisle, singing along. Lucy laughed as Paula pulled her to her feet. "That's him... that's the one I slept with. Gorgeous, isn't he?" Paula shouted, pointing to the lead singer as others around lifted their brows or their drinks toward her.

Hands in the air, dancing and laughing, Lucy gave herself over to the music, having to admit that Paula was right—the band was great and the lead singer was gorgeous.

Paula disappeared when the band left the stage, promising to be back soon. Certain that Paula was off to see if the lead singer wanted a private repeat *performance*, Lucy wandered off to find the restrooms and then meandered through the vendor stalls. She found a silversmith displaying his jewelry and bought a pair of earrings for her mother's upcoming birthday. Making her way back through the area of food trucks, she got in line for the crepes again, this time choosing one with strawberries and melted chocolate. Grabbing a handful of napkins, she devoured the treat, moaning in delight and not caring if her fingers were sticky by the end. Checking the time on her phone, she hoped Paula was back from her tryst and headed to the VIP section again, hearing the final headliner band introduced.

Arriving, she spied Paula on her feet, swaying to the music, and grinned. As she approached, her feet stumbled to a halt at the sight of who was sitting in her seat: the biker from Moose's Bar the other night.

"Lucy!" Paula screamed, her eyes wide and slightly glassy as she lurched forward, throwing her arms around her. "Look who I found! What a coincidence! I had no idea Griz was here." Paula dragged her closer, and the man stood. Much taller and bigger than she realized, Lucy's head leaned back as she took him in.

"Griz?"

"Yeah," he rumbled, his gaze penetrating while he maintained a stone-faced expression.

She licked her dry lips, not knowing what to say.

Paula giggled. "Griz is short for um… Grizzly because he… well, eats like a bear." She leaned forward, her words slurring slightly. "What he likes to eat... well, you can imagine he gives it good."

"Paula!" Lucy bit out, shifting to the side so she could speak without Griz or whoever he was listening. "You just happened to run into him? You had no idea he was here? And he's in the VIP section? Come on, how stupid do you think I am?"

"Honestly," she pouted, "I didn't know he would be here. You may have some kind of biker prejudice, but I don't."

Paula shifted her gaze over Lucy's shoulder then back again, but Lucy refused to turn around, praying Griz was keeping his distance so she could talk some sense into her friend. "Don't flip this onto me. From the patches on his jacket, I don't think he belongs to a bike club. I don't trust him."

"Well, I do."

Rearing back, she pinched her lips together. "Paula, you've had so much to drink, you're already swaying."

Paula giggled. "I know. Geoff from the band smoked a bit and then when I ran into Griz, we've had some drinks."

"What about us? You and me? Girls' day? Remember that?"

The smile fell from Paula's face. "You always want things to be about you, Lucy. Well, I want to have fun."

"And now I'm driving us home because you got high?"

"Well," Paula began, dropping her eyes to her shoes, chewing on her bottom lip. "I got a hotel room. It's not far from here."

"You got a hotel room?" Lucy didn't attempt to keep the incredulity from her voice. "We were going back tonight. Why did you get a room?"

"I'd already reserved one just in case we were tired. But Griz wants to hang out with me, and I really want to spend time with him." Paula dug around in her purse, pulling out her phone. "Here it is. It's at the Hotellerie Jardins de Ville. It's nice, honest. You can crash there tonight, and we'll head back tomorrow."

"You're ditching me? For someone you've been warned might be dangerous?"

"Christ, Lucy! Leave me alone. I'm a grown-ass woman living my life. I wanted to share a nice time with you, which we did. The drive. Lunch. The concert. Now I want to hang with someone else."

Lucy wondered if someone's head could explode from frustration, and if so, if hers was about to. Sucking in her lips, she steeled her spine, drawing herself up. "Fine. I'll go to the hotel. You do whatever. And tomorrow, we'll head home. But no more trips, Paula. No more playing your wingman."

"Oh, Lucie-goosy, don't be like that," Paula whined.

"What room?"

Huffing, Paula pulled up her phone and turned the screen around, showing the reservation. "Two-oh-three."

Jerking away, she refused to look at Griz, terrified that the scathing glare she wanted to send his way would not be taken kindly. Even if Paula had no fear, Lucy did.

The sun was setting as she used the GPS on her

phone, walked out of the park, and made her way along the sidewalks of Sherbrooke until she came to the hotel. Standing on the outside, she breathed a sigh of relief. Paula had been right, it looked nice. Not fancy, but nice.

Standing in the shadows underneath a tree, she searched her heart, trying to decide if she had been fair to Paula. *She is a grown woman. I'm not her keeper. She can do what she wants... she can do who she wants.* But no matter what she told herself, it hurt that Paula had lied, manipulated the situation, and dragged Lucy along for the company when the outcome was to meet up with Griz. *Griz for grizzly bear... Oh, my God.* Rolling her eyes, she stepped forward, marching into the lobby.

Using her basic French, she managed to get the key to room 203 with little difficulty, surprised to discover that it was already paid for. She had been so disgusted with Paula, she assumed that as the first one there, she'd have to fork over the money. Thanking the receptionist, she turned and saw the elevator next to her. The doors opened almost immediately, and she stepped in, glancing at herself in the mirrored walls. Her face registered as much irritation as she felt. Once on the second floor, she stepped out, and with a quick scan of the room number sign, walked toward the last room at the far end of the hall. Sliding her card into the lock, she stopped at the sound of motorcycles filling the evening air as a large group rolled into the parking lot.

Leaning to look down through the window next to her door at the end of the hall, she watched as a group of men climbed off their bikes, a few women with them. The men all had black leather vests and jackets, and she could see a few with the same insignia as Griz. The accompanying women appeared to be in two camps: those in similar jackets as the men—and there were only a couple of them—or those attired in skintight clothing that left nothing to the imagination. Dropping her chin to her chest, she wondered if Paula was right. *Have I become biker-prejudiced?* Forcing Paula's accusation out of her mind, she jerked her head up. *No, I'm not. My brother rides, for Christ's sake. But John didn't trust these guys, and that's good enough for me.*

Turning to the room door again, she swung the door open, ready for a hot shower and to crash onto the bed. Her feet ground to a halt at the sight in front of her. A few clothes were scattered about the room: jeans, a couple of black T-shirts, and black leather jackets with patches sewn on the back. Her gaze swept over the room and landed on the small table in the corner. Small bags of white powder, three guns, and a pile of money lay on the table. *Oh, shit!* Her heart began to pound, her breath rushing from her lungs.

The sound of shower water running in the bathroom hit her ears, and she stumbled backward. *Shit, wrong room!* Looking up at the door as she backed away in haste, she confirmed it was 203. *This is the room Paula reserved.* The water turned off, and she continued to back away quickly, her feet tripping over each other in her haste to retreat, closing the door behind her.

She looked down the hall, saw no one, and quick-walked silently over the patterned carpet toward the stairs. After passing the elevator, she heard it ding its arrival, and not trusting who might be on the elevator, she raced the last ten feet to push open the stairwell door. Heart pounding, she peeked out to observe a group of the bikers get off the elevator and walk toward the far end of the hall from where she had just come.

Her stomach dropped as she stared in stunned horror as two of the men entered room 203, hearing one of them laugh deeply as he mentioned Griz being busy that night so he wouldn't be back for a while. Lucy plastered her back against the wall, uncertain her legs would hold her upright. *It was Griz's room. Or one of his friend's rooms. Paula pawned it off on me just to get me away from her and Griz. I could've been in there. I could've been in there in the shower or the bed when those men came in. And Paula never thought about that. Or she didn't care.*

Lucy lifted her hand, her fingers fisting as they pressed against her chest, her body beginning to shake. Whether in anger or fear, rage or frustration, she had no idea. Maybe it was all of the emotions swirling inside of her. Uncertain what to do, she jolted into action, racing back down the stairs and into the lobby. More bikers were standing near the reception desk. Not wanting to be seen, she darted around a column behind a large decorative plant in a huge pot. Dropping into a chair behind the thick leaves of the plant, she grabbed a newspaper lying on a nearby table. Staying seated, she peered over the paper and between the fronds of the plant, hoping no one noticed her.

Forcing her heartbeat to slow, she sorted through various scenarios, but none of them were good. Paula knew someone would be in the room. Or Paula knew someone else could get in. Paula planned all along to meet with Griz at the concert. Did Paula know about the drugs and the guns?

Regardless of what Paula did or didn't know, Lucy was sure of one thing. *I can't wait on her to show up in the morning. I've got to get out of here!*

The lobby finally cleared as some of the bikers headed to the elevator and others called out goodbyes and left through the front door. Reaching into her bag with a still-shaking hand, she pulled out her phone.

Reading in bed, John felt restless. Lucy had been on his mind all day. He hoped she'd had a good time at the festival and had battled the desire to send her a text to tell her that. Slamming his book closed, he leaned his head back against the headboard. She might be with someone she met. Or maybe the trip wasn't just for her and Paula. He hated the images of her dancing with someone else. Being held by someone else. Being—

His phone vibrated on his nightstand and his brow furrowed at who would be calling so late. Glancing at the caller ID, his fingers squeezed his phone as he read Lucy's name. "Lucy?"

"John?"

He heard the tremor in her voice as she said his name, and his heart began to pound. Sitting up straight, he swung his legs over the side of the bed. "Lucy? What's wrong? What's happening?"

"I don't know what to do. I'm so sorry to call, but you're the person I thought of when…"

Her words tapered off, managing to send his heartbeat skyrocketing. Standing, he held the phone between his shoulder and ear, jerking his jeans up his legs. "Just tell me. What the hell is happening?"

"It started fine, everything with Paula was great. But she lied to me. By this evening, she'd met up with that biker that she'd been sitting with at the bar the other night—"

"Goddamnit!" She grew quiet, and he hated that his curse had probably scared her. Calming his voice, he prodded, "Keep going, please."

"We were going to come back tonight, but she wants to spend the night with him. She told me she had a hotel room for us, which makes me wonder if she ever planned on us coming back tonight. Anyway, she said since she was going off with him then I could have the room, and we'd come back tomorrow morning. I was pissed but I walked to the hotel, and it seemed nice. A whole group of bikers pulled into the parking lot and are staying here in the hotel. But when I got up to my room, it was already being used. There was a biker jacket, guns, money, and I think drugs out on the table, and someone was in the shower. I got out of there before anyone could see me. John, it was never just for her and me. It was some kind of biker group room, I guess—"

"Goddamn, fuckin' bitch!" He lost his cool again. He squeezed his eyes tightly shut, giving his head a shake. He was known for his cool head, his calm demeanor. That's what made him perfect for demolitions. But right now, he was ready to explode. "Tell me where you are, I'm coming to get you."

"No, John, you don't have to come here. It'll take you four hours to get here and by then... oh, I don't know."

"By then what, Lucy? Paula will show up? Who will she have with her?" Her end of the line was quiet, and then he heard the unmistakable sound of a soft gasp. *Shit... I'm a fuckin' ass to scare her more than she is.* He sighed heavily. "Lucy, please, don't cry. Please. I'm sorry. I'm not trying to make things worse."

"No, it's not you. It's me. Actually, it's not even me. It's her and them! I'm angry, and I'm tired, and I'm scared. But I don't want you to have to come to get me. I'm just out of my element and wanted you to tell me what you think I should do."

Forcing his heart rate to slow and his breathing to even out, he put her on speaker as he set his phone on his nightstand, giving his arms freedom to jerk on a long-sleeved T-shirt and jam his feet into his boots. "I'm coming. Period. No discussion and no guilt. I don't think you're safe and it's killing me that you're four hours away. This is what I want you to do. Is there any other place around that you can get to that will keep you in a well-lit area?"

"Um... there was a diner next to the hotel, but some of the bikers were heading out to the parking lot in that direction."

"You want to stay away from there. Anywhere else?" He grabbed his wallet and his keys and headed downstairs. He scribbled a note to his grandfather, explaining that he needed to go pick up a friend and wouldn't be back until the next day.

"Honestly, John, I think I'm as safe as I can be right here in the lobby. It's well-lit and there are several hotel employees behind the desk. I'm in a corner, hidden, and I don't think anyone will bother me here."

"Okay, I want you to text me the address, and I'll be on the road in five minutes. This time of night I can get there faster. If anything happens, you call the police. Under no circumstances do you go off with anyone, and that includes Paula. You stay exactly where you are, understand?"

"Yes, yes. I'll stay right here."

"Okay, I'm on my way—"

"John?"

"Yeah, babe?"

Her voice hitched. "Thank you."

"No, thank you for calling me. And Lucy? Stay safe. I'm coming for you."

He was in his SUV, had his GPS set for the destination, and was on the road in three minutes, then two minutes later, he called Bray.

"What's up, man?"

"Got a situation." His words were clipped, and he could hear Bray's immediate attention with his offer.

"Shit, you need backup?"

"No. Just didn't want to fuck up my chances with Mace but also don't know how this is going to go down."

"Talk to me."

He gave Bray the fast version of Lucy's situation,

ending with, "I'm going to get her. I don't plan on any problems, but her safety is of utmost importance."

"Okay, listen, John. I'll tell you what Mace always tells us when we're first hired. Remember, you no longer represent the United States government. The good thing is you don't have their rules to follow, but you also don't have the protection of being a soldier following orders. And since you're not an official LSI Keeper, you don't have Mace's protection either. At least, not officially."

"Got it. Shouldn't need it, but I understand."

"But listen, you're not alone. Get to her, drive safe, and don't engage. Just get her out and get back here. While you're driving, I'm calling it into Mace and briefing the others. Josh and Rick can call up the CCTV to give you insight into the area if needed. Mace can call in markers if needed also. But I'll tell you this—keep your eyes open. Whatever intel you can gather and bring back on the Minotaurs, we can use."

"You got it."

Bray explained the border procedure for a civilian before they disconnected, and for the first time in the past fifteen minutes, his breathing eased slightly. He thought of Mace, Bray, and the others. Teamwork. Just like old times. Just what he missed.

Looking at his GPS, he turned on the radio. At this speed... three hours to go.

Approaching the hotel's parking lot at almost three a.m., John's attention was razor-sharp. He saw the bikes parked in the lot, and driving slowly, pulled out his phone, snapping the license plates of several of them. Parking to the side, he approached the well-lit lobby and saw several more bikers milling around on the inside. He entered the glass doors and glanced around. His gaze swung side to side, but he didn't see Lucy. His stomach dropped and his heart pounded, but he kept his expression blank when the bored receptionist looked his way.

Turning, he spied a chair in the corner, well-hidden behind a plant. Moving forward, it was obvious there was no one there. *Fuckin' hell.* His phone vibrated in his pocket. Pulling it out, he read the text.

Outside. Near your vehicle.

Fighting the urge to run, he turned and walked outside, making his way to his SUV, careful to stay in the shadows and keep his eye out for anyone, Lucy or biker, not knowing if she sent the text or if someone had her and was using her phone to lure him out. Approaching his vehicle from the rear, he stopped, his head cocked to the side, listening.

A movement caught his attention as a head popped up over the hood of his SUV.

"John?" came the soft female voice he'd already memorized.

He hustled forward, barely able to plant his feet as Lucy ran, slamming into him as her arms encircled his waist. "Christ, Lucy," he managed to get out, finding his breath stuck in his lungs at the feel of her shaking body pressed against his as though she were burrowing to be as close as possible. Wrapping her up, he buried his nose in her hair, pulling her tight with one hand on the back of her head and the other banded across her back. Until he had her in his arms, he'd refused to acknowledge how worried he'd been. Now, all the emotions threatened to rush to the forefront, a problem he'd never dealt with before on a mission.

Her arm stayed locked tightly around him, and in another time or place he'd want nothing more than to enjoy her silky hair against his skin, breathe in her scent, and revel in the feel of her luscious body pressed against his, but they needed to get out of there and back home.

Leaning back, he looked down. "Lucy, it's okay. I'm here. But why the fuck did you not stay inside?"

She tilted her head back, tears shimmering in her eyes. "I didn't think it was safe."

Unable to keep the reproach from his expression, he shook his head. "Lucy."

Her fingers clutched tighter to the back of his shirt as she shifted her gaze from side to side before bringing it back to his face. Her words came out in a rush, a tremor in her voice. "No, you don't understand. It was fine for a while, and then suddenly, the stairwell door near me flew open and several of them came out. My chair was kind of behind the door so nobody paid any attention to me, but the lobby was beginning to be a gathering place. I thought they'd all gone up and gone to bed, but it's like they don't sleep. By then, there was only the one person behind the reception desk, and believe me, John, if anything was going to happen, they'd do nothing. They didn't look scared, so it made me wonder if this group hasn't come here before. But I knew beyond a shadow of a doubt that if anyone started bothering me, I was not going to get any help. So, I slipped out of the lobby and went through the back door. I've been hiding in the bushes over there until you got here."

"Fuckin' hell, babe." He was torn between admiration for her keeping a cool head and rage that she felt threatened. *If I get my hands on fuckin' Paula...* "Okay, that's done, and we're out of here." The parking lot was quiet, but he didn't trust it would stay that way for long. Opening the passenger door, he ushered her in, hating the sight of her hands shaking so badly she was barely able to handle the seatbelt. "Let me." He adjusted it around her, clicking it in place. Her hair was askance, completely falling out of the clip at the top of her head. Her green top was wrinkled, and her blue jeans had a bit of dirt on the knees.

Leaning forward, with his face directly in front of hers, he wanted to fill her sight with only him. Her eyes were wide, and he placed his lips on her forehead. Mumbling against her soft skin, he vowed, "You're safe, and I'm taking you out of here." Closing the door, he hustled around the front and climbed in.

Starting the engine, he drove around the back of the hotel and pulled out into the alley before turning onto the road. Lucy's hands were clasped tightly in front of her, her fingers wrapped around the strap of her backpack. He tapped a button on his phone. As soon as the line connected, he said, "I've got her. She's safe. Leaving now."

"Good job, congratulations. Take the time you need, then we'd like a report."

"You got it." He disconnected.

He felt her stare against the side of his head but simply reached to the console and pulled out a water bottle, handing it to her. "Drink."

She acquiesced and drank deeply. With each swallow, her body appeared to relax. They remained quiet until they passed out of the city limits, and then her breathing seemed to ease.

Once they crossed the border into the United States with no difficulty, he heard her massive although shaky sigh of relief. He thought he did a better job of hiding his, but the truth was he'd sighed as well.

13

"You're exhausted, Lucy. Why don't you close your eyes and try to get some sleep?"

"I know I should, but I don't want to. When I close my eyes, I feel yukky. Sick with anger, nerves, frustration. We've got at least three hours to go. I'd rather stay awake and talk to you."

"Are you sure?"

"Yeah. I feel a lot better having some water, and to be honest, as soon as we crossed over the border, I feel like there's less of a threat. I suppose that's silly, but..."

"No, it's not silly at all. Certainly, their reach can be far, but we should be safe."

She shifted in her seat, twisting more to face him. "Can I ask who you were reporting to?"

He kept his eyes on the road, occasionally glancing to the side, finding her attention focused directly on him. "I told you that I had a lead on a job in security. I've met with them, and it looks like that's going to move forward and I'll become an employee. I'm not on their payroll yet, but it turns out that I knew one of them from the military. So, after you called, I felt it was prudent to let someone know what was happening."

"So, you called your friend? The one who works for the security company?"

"Yes. And he let the others know what was happening. They had the resources that helped me get to you quicker."

She reached over and placed her hand on his arm. "I had no idea anyone else would be involved."

With one hand still on the steering wheel, he reached over and gave her hand a squeeze. "I can handle things on my own, but it felt better to have a team behind me. Plus, I wanted to make sure what I was walking into. I'm used to planning missions before going in, and as much as I wanted to get to you, I had to know what the threat was."

"Who are they, John?"

"The Minotaurs are an outlaw biker gang that run drugs and guns in Canada, sometimes making their way down across the border. The Hell's Angels have taken over most of the biker gangs in Canada, but for some reason, with the Minotaurs, they formed a partnership."

Lucy didn't say anything, and he swung his head to the side, searching her expression. She turned her face back toward the windshield, her mouth opened as she sputtered before finally forming words. "And this is who Paula has literally gotten in bed with?"

"I don't know what to tell you. If she knows what

they are and what they're doing, then as far as I'm concerned, she's an accessory to everything that was going on. If she thinks she's just playing on the wild side, then she's going to get burned, and I'm fuckin' pissed that she's willing to let you get burned also. And if she doesn't think there's anything wrong with her behavior—or theirs—then she really is stupid."

"I don't even want to think about her right now." Lucy remained quiet for a few minutes, finally sighing heavily and leaning her head against the headrest. She pulled out her phone and looked at the screen. "She hasn't even texted me. Hasn't asked how I am, or if she made it to the hotel, asked where I am." Looking over at him, she asked, "What do I do?"

It was on the tip of his tongue to say 'fuck her', but he pinched his lips together for a few seconds. "Send her a text and tell her that you called a friend to pick you up and that you're heading home."

Her fingers tapped out the message. "Anything else?"

"No. Don't engage. Don't accuse, don't ask why. If she texts you back, don't reply."

She shoved her phone back into her bag and dropped it onto the floorboard near her feet.

"I hate to make you go into more details, but when you can, I need to know what you saw. I want to call this in so you only have to go over it once. Can you do that?" She nodded, but he pushed. "Lucy, I want to hear you say it."

"Yes, John. I'll tell you and... um... whoever I need to about what I saw. No one knows I was in the room, so it can't be traced back to me. Well, I don't think it can. I guess that depends on if Paula told anyone that I might be there." She lifted her hand to her forehead. "God, all this gives me a headache." Sucking in a deep breath, she nodded as she looked at him. "Okay, let's do this."

Using the number he'd been given, he called Bray. "She's ready to talk."

"Okay, good. Um... Lucy? I'm a friend of John's, and you're on speaker with some coworkers of mine. We just need to know what you saw."

He glanced to the side, seeing her lips pull in, and her eyes sought his. Reaching over, he held her hand. "Just talk like you're talking to me, Lucy. It's fine, I promise."

"O... okay," she said, haltingly at first. She kept her face toward him as he continued to hold her hand. She quickly described what had happened at the concert and how she ended up at the hotel. "There was a leather bag on the bed that looked kind of like a large backpack. That was what I noticed first. It was open and there were some clothes scattered... a pair of jeans, a couple of T-shirts. There was a black leather jacket tossed on the bed as well. That's when I saw the same insignia as what Griz had worn. I was in shock that I had possibly been given the wrong room key and just stood there for a few seconds trying to make sense of it all."

Prodding, John asked, "What else was in the room? On the table."

She licked her lips and said, "There was a beer bottle. A stack of money... like you see in movies where the bills were rubber-banded together. I have no idea how much or what denominations, but there were at least four or five banded stacks. I saw three guns… um, I don't know anything about guns, but they were hand-guns. And then there were several plastic baggies like you put sandwiches in and they were filled with white powder. I assumed drugs, but I can't say for sure."

"Lucy, you're doing great," Bray said. "The most important thing is that you're safe, and John's got you and bringing you home. He's the best and you're in good hands."

John's chest swelled with pride hearing Bray's commendation, but he gave her hand another squeeze. "Got to tell you all that the real hero is Lucy. She kept her cool, called me, stayed off their radar, and even hid when she thought she might be discovered. Honest to God, she's amazing."

Bray chuckled and added, "Then Lucy, our hats are off to you. Now, get some sleep and let John take care of everything."

The call disconnected, and for several minutes, they traveled down the dark road, the black forest on either side pressing in with only the headlights in front of them providing illumination. He wondered if she was falling asleep, hoping she would rest but wishing they'd had more time to talk.

She shifted again, then said, "Your friend is right. You really are my hero, you know. I'd love to know more about you, John, but the last time I asked it didn't go so well."

A heavy sigh left his lips, and he winced at the memory. "Lucy, I'm sorry. I was an ass."

She barked out a combination snort-laugh and shook her head. "You were not an ass."

He thought the sound of her laughter was adorable and would have disagreed with her assessment but was glad she was giving him another chance. He hated talking about himself but knew if he was ever going to have a chance with her, he needed to get over his fuckin' hang-ups and talk. "It's been hard coming back home the way I did. I've been home to visit but never home to stay. Considering it wasn't by choice, at least not initially, I was struggling."

"So, Maine was a place you came to because of your grandparents?"

"Yeah. As an Army family, we moved around a lot, but Mom couldn't hack it. My parents were young when they got married, had me just two years later. I think Mom thought it was going to be exciting being married to someone in the Army. A chance to travel and see new places. I think she was ready to escape the little town she grew up in. That happened, but I can remember my parents fighting almost every time we had to pack up and move. Mom would cry and want to know why we couldn't stay somewhere longer. She cried when we got to a place and said she didn't know anyone and didn't have any friends. She cried and said she was tired of packing and unpacking, tired of on-base housing or trying to find an apartment some-where. And then Dad would get called up for an over-seas duty that was unaccompanied and be gone for six to twelve months." He sighed, scrubbing his hand over his face. "I think I struggled for many years with her unhappiness. I used to think that I should have been able to do something to make her happier, but she was unhappy in her marriage and unhappy with her life."

"No, John. You were just a child. And it's not a child's responsibility to make their parent's life happy."

"I know she loved me, but it just wasn't enough."

Lucy's hand landed on his leg, her voice heavy. "Oh, I'm so sorry you carry the burden that was never yours to carry."

He dropped his right hand to hers, and she twisted her fingers around to link through his. As difficult as the topic of conversation was, the feel of her palm against his warmed him straight through to his heart.

"To be honest, I don't think it's that uncommon for military families. All the kids I knew were constantly moving, and I knew more than one whose parents split up. But I had no idea that's what Mom was thinking of until I was about ten years old and she simply left. I came home from school and saw her packing and wondered if we were having another move. I asked her where we were going and she looked up, tears in her eyes, and told me that *we* weren't going anywhere but *she* needed a break. I thought maybe she was going to visit relatives, but she left and didn't come back."

Lucy's fingers flexed against his. "I simply can't imagine that. My family wasn't perfect, but my parents love each other and made sure that my brother and I knew that. But what a horrible thing for her to do to you."

"I struggled with it for many years. I ended up spending more and more time with my grandparents, and it was my grandmother who finally explained to me that none of this was my fault. She said my mom was a good woman who simply had been very unhappy as a military wife. So unhappy that she felt the only thing she could do was leave."

Lucy shook her head, angry vibes coming from her. "I don't understand. She didn't just leave her marriage. She left her child! I can't even believe that. To leave and not have a continued relationship with you." She heaved out a breath that sounded a lot like righteous indignation. "Can I ask where she is now?"

"I used to ask about her but my dad just said he didn't know. It was my grandmother who told me several years later that Mom had died of breast cancer. She'd remarried but never had more children."

"Oh... now I'm even more sorry. How tragic for everyone. How did your dad deal?"

Thinking for a moment, John tried to mesh his thoughts with his memories. "My dad was a good guy but he was gone a lot. I don't know what kind of relationship we would've had if he had lived, but I'd like to think that we would have forged some kind of friendship, at least based on mutual military service. But as a ten-year-old kid, he was angry that Mom left and that it made things a lot harder for him. Sometimes, I wondered if anyone even saw me." He had no idea where that last sentence came from, having never verbalized that thought before, but somehow, with Lucy, it was so easy to talk.

"You stayed quiet, hoping if you didn't rock the boat, your Mom would be happier. And then you stayed quiet, not wanting to rock the boat to make things easier on your dad."

He nodded, rubbing his thumb over her fingers. "I think you're right." He glanced at a road sign for an upcoming town and said, "We'll find an all-night gas station. We can go to the restroom, grab some food, and I can fill up the SUV."

Nodding, she smiled as she pulled her hand away, and the cool air swept over his palm as he immediately missed her warm touch. It only took five minutes for him to find an open convenience store. He filled the tank before escorting her inside. He checked the hall and nodded for her to enter the ladies' room. "I'll be right here."

She soon finished her business and stepped back into the hall. Her hair had been pulled into a messy bun held by a large clip, and her face was bright, a few water droplets still visible on her neck.

He inclined his head toward the men's room. "Stay here, and I'll be out in just a moment." She followed his directions, smiling as he approached a few minutes later. "Let's get some food."

She lifted a brow and teased, "Junk food?"

Chuckling, he wrapped his arm around her shoulder. "Get whatever you want. I'll grab a couple of their breakfast bagels since it seems like they just made some."

"Ooh, that sounds good. I'll get the coffee."

She moved to the coffee station and began fixing

two cups while he ordered breakfast bagels with egg, cheese, and bacon. Paying for everything, they had just made it to the car when the sound of a motorcycle roaring down the street met their ears. She startled, almost dropping the coffee, a gasp rushing from her lips as her wide-eyed, fear-filled gaze shot up to his. The bike continued past and John kept his eyes on it until it was out of sight. Looking down, he said, "Breathe, Lucy. It was no one."

The air left her lungs and she nodded, mumbling, "Sorry."

He assisted her into the SUV, then climbed in, handing her the bag of food. "You've got nothing to be sorry for. So far, you've handled yourself perfectly." She offered a smile, and he pulled onto the road, letting her unwrap the bagels to give her something to focus on.

They ate in silence, and when finished, he glanced to the side as she took the wrapper from his and wadded it up, placing it into the bag. "You gonna be able to sleep now?"

She laughed, shaking her head. "Now I'm jazzed up on coffee." After a moment, she turned back to him and asked, "Will you keep talking? Tell me about your dad and then your grandparents?"

He reached out, laying his hand on the console, palm up. It was a simple invitation, and as soon as her fingers linked with his again, he smiled. Once again, the feel of her hand in his sent warmth throughout his body. "I spent the next couple of years in the schools on our base and the summers in Maine with my grandparents. Dad did not get another overseas assignment during that time, and I couldn't help but think that he sometimes resented the chains of being a single father. When I was thirteen, in Maine for the summer, he was on a training mission in California. There was an accident and his vehicle rolled down an embankment. I remember the man who came to the door to inform my grandparents that my dad had been killed."

"Just when I think your story can't get any worse, it does," Lucy said. "And I feel like I've said 'I'm sorry' constantly, but I truly am."

"Thanks, but it was a long time ago. Fuckin' gutted me at the time, but after twenty years, I just hang on to my good memories and don't agonize about what could have been."

"That sounds pretty wise. Why do I get the feeling that perhaps your grandparents helped teach you that?"

Laughing, he said, "Just wait till you meet my grandfather. He's a goodhearted man, but he believes in moving on through life no matter what it throws at you."

"I hope I do get to meet him." She leaned closer, her eyes lit by the lights from the dashboard.

If they were anywhere other than the middle-of-the-road, he'd close the distance and kiss her. Clearing his throat, he nodded. "Then I'll make sure you do."

"So, that's how you made Maine your home."

"Yep. My mom was still living but there was no way I was going to go live with her. So, my grandparents became my guardians, and I spent the next five years with them. My grandfather was the silent type, my grandmother was full of laughter and love. They were opposites, and yet it worked. It was during those years that I got bigger, played sports, did okay in school, and my grandparents made sure to give me unconditional love. But by the time I graduated, I wanted to join the Army. I suppose psychiatrists would have a field day with that decision, saying that I was trying to get close to my deceased father or trying to recreate my childhood. The fact of the matter was I didn't want to go to college, I didn't have a particular career I was interested in, and the Army had a place for me."

"You talk about your grandfather, but..."

What she was trying to ask sent a squeeze to his chest, more than talking about his mom or his dad. "My grandmother died about ten years ago. Since then, it's just been my grandfather."

"And now you since you're home to stay."

"Yeah, and now me."

He glanced at the map on the SUV's computer screen. "We don't have far to go."

Lucy shifted again, her head still facing him but resting against the seat. She yawned widely, her hand lifted to pat her lips.

"You should go to sleep," he encouraged. "It's after five a.m."

"But what about you? I need to keep you talking so that you don't fall asleep behind the wheel."

A rueful bark of laughter erupted. "I haven't talked this much about myself in... in... hell, ever!"

"Well, good," she mumbled, yawning again. "I like learning more about you."

"Why?" The question slipped out unbidden, and he winced, wishing he could pull it back.

The silence in the SUV was no longer comfortable but charged with electricity that seemed to zap about the space. She remained quiet for several minutes, and he thought perhaps she'd gone to sleep until she finally spoke.

He came for me. If nothing else, I owe him honesty. Lucy spoke, her voice soft, barely above a whisper. "I was so excited to have a local soldier that the class could write to. It was supposed to be a lesson for the children, combining history, current events, and community service. I had no idea if someone would write back but was thrilled when you did. After I sent you a picture of the class and in your next letter you sent one of you and some of your buddies, I was... I felt..."

Her voice trailed off, words failing her. John said nothing, and she struggled to gather her thoughts and speak, the heat of self-consciousness burning in her gut.

"It was a picture of you and four of your buddies, but I didn't need to look at the back of the photograph where you'd indicated which one was you. Just looking at the picture, I knew. It was your eyes. Your expression. The others were all laughing, and while you were also smiling, it was more serious. Your sunglasses were pushed up to the top of your head, and while I know you were staring at the camera, it felt as though you were staring at me. Before I put the picture up on our bulletin board in our classroom, I had a copy made. One just for me."

She shook her head, an embarrassed chuckle slipping from her lips. "Jesus, saying it aloud makes me sound like I have some kind of adolescent crush." Sucking in a deep breath, she let it out slowly, her words barely audible, confessing, "Maybe I do."

She was quiet for a moment, then pulled her bravery around like a cape. Twisting around to see his face in profile, she continued her admission. "I think I looked forward to your letters even more than the children did, and believe me, they were very excited. I wanted to know how you were, what you were doing, and I... I began to care greatly."

He shot her a smile, so she pressed onward. "That's why I reacted so bizarrely in the hardware store. I didn't know it was you. I just thought you looked really similar to John Roster. And since you were someone that I'd spent a lot of time thinking about, well, seeing someone who looked like you had me tripping over my own feet. Then I was shocked when you came into the classroom, sure that I would probably never meet you in person. I know we started as pen pals but hoped we could become friends." She hefted her shoulders in a little shrug. "So, as horrible as the reason for this trip, I'm glad I had the chance to get to know you better."

Afraid he was going to think she was either desperate or a stalker—or perhaps a desperate stalker— she sat perfectly still, uncertain what else to do or say.

He reached over and placed his hand on hers, and her breath left her lungs slowly, afraid too much movement would make him pull away.

"I'm glad for the chance, too," he said, glancing toward her, his eyes just as dark and intense as his photograph.

She allowed herself a small smile and leaned her head against the headrest again. Making her confession and not being rejected, her heart stopped squeezing. She would still have to deal with Paula but for now refused to think about her, focusing instead on John.

Yawning widely again as the early morning sun began to streak rays of light across the sky, she was glad to see that they were nearing her home. He pulled to a stop next to her vehicle, still parked in front of her house. She wanted to ask him in, but he'd given so much of his time. She simply leaned down and grabbed her bag, unbuckled her seatbelt, and turned to thank him, but he had already thrown open his door and was stalking around the front of his SUV to her side. He offered his hand and assisted her down. She opened her mouth again to thank him, but he threw his arm around her shoulder and walked her to her front door. She dug around in her bag and pulled out her keys, jiggling them in the lock until the door swung open. Once more she turned to thank him, but he ushered her inside, closing the door behind him, standing close, his gaze burning intensely as he stared down at her.

Blinking in surprise, she wasn't sure if she should offer him something to eat, the use of her bathroom before he got back on the road to go to his house, or if he'd like to crash on her couch and sleep for a few hours. *Or my bed with me would be preferable, but I'd better keep that to myself.* No words came forth as she stared up at him.

His hand lifted and he cupped her jaw. She remained motionless as his thumb swept over the apple of her cheek. Swallowing deeply, her breath was shallow as she continued to stare up into his eyes. He bent, ever so slowly, giving her plenty of opportunities to back away, shake her head, tell him 'no'. Instead, she lifted slightly onto her toes, drawn to him.

His face filled her view, so much so she was unable to see or process anything other than the warmth in his eyes as his gaze captured her completely. Erasing the minuscule space between them, his lips landed on hers. The kiss started light, the barest wisp of a touch. He nibbled on her upper lip before the tip of his tongue danced along the seam of her lips. Opening her mouth in a silent but hopeful invitation, her belly swooshed as his tongue slid inside, tangling with hers as it explored.

Her fingers clenched his shoulders, bunching the material of his shirt in her grip, and his arm banded tightly around her middle, pressing her front to his. The kiss never flamed wild and hot, not like she knew it could, but instead filled her senses, letting her know the attraction and longing weren't one-sided. She angled her head, wanting more, deeper, everything, but he pulled back slightly.

Opening her eyes, she wanted to howl in protest at the loss of his mouth on hers, but his lips curved and the sight captured and held her attention. Everything she had seen in his photograph... the calm, quiet, reserved, loyal, duty-bound, dedicated friend and soldier was still there, just now in the flesh and pressed against her.

"Stay," she whispered, the word pulled from the depths of her soul.

He said nothing. Embarrassed, her fingers started to unclench their grip on his shoulders.

"You need to sleep." His words were guttural, almost tortured.

Licking her kiss-swollen lips, she pressed onward. "So, stay. Stay and sleep." She watched as his gaze shot toward her living room, and without turning her head to see that he'd focused on her small sofa, she continued. "Sleep with me. Just sleep. My house may be a wreck, but my bed is comfortable. We can sleep for a couple of hours, and I'll fix you a real breakfast when we wake."

Again, he remained quiet, and she could tell nothing of his thoughts. Relaxing her stance, she started to step back only to find his grip tightening. Her breath halted, her fingers flexing at the feel of his hands on her.

"Yeah."

A slow smile curved her lips. "Yeah?"

His face was transformed as his slight smile met hers. "Yeah." His hand slid from her back to her arm, trailing a path as he reached her hand and linked fingers. Turning, he led her down the short hall, allowing her to move into her bedroom first.

She stepped inside, nerves making her stomach flutter. Looking around, she had no idea what to do. *Change into PJs. Pull the covers down. Ask if he wanted a spare toothbrush.*

"Stop worrying," he ordered, his voice gentle, giving her hand a little tug to draw her attention back to his face. "You've had enough worry to deal with." He inclined his head toward the bathroom. "Take care of what you need. Get comfortable. I'll send a couple of texts, and then when you're finished, I'll do the same. Then we'll grab a couple of hours of sleep. Yeah?"

Nodding, she was glad he was able to so succinctly voice what she needed to focus on. "Yeah." Turning, she hustled into the bathroom and took the fastest shower she'd ever had, all the time trying—and failing—to not think of John Roster in her bedroom while she was naked. Braiding her long, wet hair, she moisturized and brushed her teeth. Unearthing an extra toothbrush from the ones given to her by the dentist, she laid it next to the sink, then stepped out wearing pajama bottoms and a sleep T-shirt.

Her feet stumbled at the sight of John, his hip leaning casually against her dresser, the man she'd daydreamed about for months.

He looked up from his phone and sent his gaze moving from her wet hair down to her bare toes and back again. Grinning, he kissed the top of her head as he passed her and headed into the bathroom. Blowing out a breath, she walked to her bed, hesitated for just a few seconds, and then jerked the covers back and climbed into bed. The shower started again, and now she tried—and failed—to think of anything but a naked John Roster.

Yawning, she glanced at the clock, knowing she had been awake for twenty-four hours, and wondered if she could sleep. She yawned again, her eyes growing heavy, the worry and fatigue of her misadventures having sapped her energy. Blinking scratchy eyes, she decided to make sure she was on her half of the bed before he came out and curled up on her side, fluffed the pillow, and closed her eyes as she waited for him.

Then she fell asleep.

John stood in front of the bathroom mirror, a towel about his waist, unable to believe that he was still in her house. *I should drive home. Sleep in my own bed. Check on Gramps.* But the sight of Lucy staring up at him, so strong in the face of a difficult and dangerous situation, her eyes pleading as she whispered 'Stay', was more than he could bear. Snorting, he shook his head. *My team would laugh their asses off to hear me say that I didn't have the ability to walk away from her again.* But it didn't matter. He'd made that mistake once and wasn't going to do it again.

He pulled his boxers back on and flipped off the light. Stepping into the bedroom, his gaze shot to the bed and he chuckled lightly. He padded on silent footsteps to the side and looked down. Her dark hair was pulled back but tendrils created a halo about her face on the pillow. Her breathing was deep and slow. For another few seconds, he considered slipping out and letting her sleep in peace, but instead, he slid underneath the covers, staying carefully on his side. *Her house might be a wreck but her mattress was amazing.*

He lay on his back for a moment, afraid to move, almost afraid to breathe, not wanting to do anything to disturb her. While he'd been awake as long as she had, his body was more used to getting little sleep. When finally convinced that she was not waking, he gently rolled to the side away from her to turn out the lamp on the nightstand.

His hand halted in midair as his gaze landed on the photograph staring back at him. Five teammates, friends, comrades with their arms around each other, cocky grins and ass-kicking stances. Emotions crashed into him, each vying for dominance as they pushed to the forefront of his mind.

The day the picture was taken. A mission accomplished. Hard-fought but easily won. Like almost all their missions, successful.

The guys in the picture. Leibowitz, Roselli, Smithwick, Johnson... *and me in the middle.* An ache formed in his chest at the stark realization that he would never again be part of *that* team, never have another picture with *those* men, four of the best men he'd ever known.

He turned his head ever so slowly toward the right, watching as the black spot in his peripheral vision finally obliterated the photograph on the nightstand. His teeth ground together before he twisted his head back, staring at the picture once again.

His phone vibrated, and he grabbed it so the noise would not wake Lucy. Glancing at the screen, he saw two messages had come in. The first one was from Bray.

Glad you're back. Boss will be in touch. I'll buy you a round of beer next time we're out.

He couldn't help but smile, figuring that with the help the Keepers had given, he would owe all of them a round of beer.

The next message came from Mace.

Good work. Rest. Make sure Lucy is safe. Come in tomorrow morning to debrief. Paperwork will come in today.

His smile widened with the knowledge that first thing Monday morning he'd go into the LSI headquarters. On top of that, he'd already had a chance to work with and—hopefully—convince his new boss and coworkers that he could handle the job.

He laid his phone back down on the nightstand next to the photograph, offering a silent chin lift to the image of his old friends. For what they were, what they had been, what they meant to him and always would. But he now felt lighter knowing there was a future beyond the Army.

Lucy stirred beside him, and he looked over his shoulder to see her shift around, facing him but still asleep. Her complexion was pale, her eyelashes forming crescents that rested on her cheeks. A few freckles crossed over her nose, barely visible, and yet he fought to keep his finger from reaching out to trace them. Her lips were full, and now he knew just how kissable they were.

He thought back to her confession. She'd felt something the first time she had seen his picture. He now wished that she'd been in the photograph of the class so that he could have spent the last eight months staring at her, but he couldn't deny how right everything felt now.

He reached his hand over and finished what he'd started several minutes ago by turning out the light. The room fell into semi-darkness, early morning sunlight peeking through the blinds as he settled on his side, facing her. Leaning forward, he kissed her forehead lightly, wondering if he'd be able to sleep next to her without pulling her into his arms.

A few minutes later, she snuggled closer to him, and with her cheek resting against his shoulder, he fell asleep.

15

Lucy blinked open her eyes, the sunlight much brighter in her bedroom than normal. Her pillow was much firmer than usual and something heavy rested over her waist and leg. Squeezing her eyes shut before opening them again in an effort to see clearer, all that met her gaze was the smooth skin, flat nipples, and defined abs that were presented before her. Sucking in a hasty breath, she lifted her head slightly and peered down.

With John's dark hair sticking up slightly on top and his face relaxed in slumber, he was just as gorgeous as the first time she'd looked at his picture but now had a boyish quality she'd never seen. The truth was she'd fallen for a man she only knew through letters and a photograph, willing to admit that was premature and somewhat based on fantasies. But the more she got to know him, the more she realized her initial assessment was right... he was a good man through and through.

His eyes shot open, and a squeak slipped through her lips as she startled.

"Sorry," he mumbled, his hand reaching out for hers. "Force of habit. I wake quickly, especially if I sense I'm not in a familiar place."

"I woke a few minutes ago and couldn't figure out why my pillow felt so hard. I'm afraid I was laying on your shoulder."

He moved his leg and blushed. "It seems I had you trapped down. Guess I wasn't so good at staying on my side."

"Me either," she laughed.

His hand lifted slowly, gently tucking wayward strands of hair behind her ear. "I want to kiss you good morning. Is that okay?"

Her lips curved, and she nodded. "Yeah," she said, leaning closer as his hand slid to the back of her head.

Their legs remained tangled and now their chests were pressed together as he gently pulled her toward him, their mouths sealing. Steel and silk. Soft and strong. Light nibbles that became tongues dancing. She sighed into his mouth, and he groaned, his fingers flexing, tugging her hair. He tore his lips from her mouth and kissed along her cheek, nibbling on her earlobe. She slid one hand into his hair, her trimmed nails scratching along his scalp.

Trailing kisses down her neck, he sucked lightly at the pulse point, and she shivered. The whoosh that moved through her body from her lips to her sex had her shifting her hips forward, his erection tucked against her tummy.

His hand slid down, his fingers gripping her hip. Lifting his head from her neck, his gaze penetrated the lust fog she was lost in. "I want you, Lucy, but not today."

Her chest heaved as her breath left her quickly, but he didn't give her a chance to protest or convince him they needed to get naked.

"Honestly, babe, I want you. I want you naked and under me. And this is killing me to pull back, but there's no way I'm going to take advantage of what's happening. Yesterday was a shit-kicker for you. Plus, you've only had a couple of hours of sleep, and you're still dealing and reeling from all that happened."

She sucked in her still-tingling lips, her hand resting lightly on his cheek. His gaze was warm, his eyes searching. Her head nodded slowly, and she smiled. "You really are a good man, John Roster."

A chuckle erupted from deep inside his chest, the rumble moving against her body. She thought it might be one of her favorite sounds—right after the groan he made when his tongue invaded her mouth.

"As much as I'd love to stay in bed with you, I know eventually I'd stop being a good man when the temptation overtook my best intentions. So, we're gonna get up, get dressed, have something to eat, and plan our date."

She blinked, her chin jerking back. "Our date?"

"Hell, yeah, our date. I fucked up when I walked away from you before, and I'm not going to make that mistake again. But we've had a second chance, even if that came from a bad place for you. So, I'm going to start over, and we're going to have a date."

"A date," she repeated, her smile widening as the belly whoosh moved through her again. "I'd like that."

His smile lit her room, and she pushed against his shoulder to raise up to sit on the bed. "Okay, then it's breakfast and date planning. That sounds perfect to me!"

She stayed in her sleep shorts and t-shirt, but he pulled on his jeans over his boxers before they moved into the kitchen. While she scrambled eggs and made French toast, she caught him looking around. "I worked on the kitchen and bathrooms first," she said. "I knew I needed a place to take a shower, and I had to have food."

"Sounds like your plan was solid."

"It's not finished, of course. But it's functional." She plated the food and they sat at the table they'd been at before... *just before he went silent and then left so abruptly.* Staring down at her plate, she wondered if he would turn cold again, and doubt crept over her.

"Hey." He placed his hand over hers, dragging her attention up to him. "What are you thinking about that put such a frown on your face?"

Lifting her head, she stared at him. Rugged handsomeness stared back, but she could observe concern in his eyes. "I was just wondering what happened before. You know... when you were here, and I thought things were going well, and then you left so quickly." She watched his shoulders fall slightly and rushed, "You don't have to tell me. You don't—"

"No, Lucy, stop. Don't apologize and backtrack. If we're starting something, then we need to be honest.

You need to be able to ask what you want, and I need to get over my shit and be honest."

"Oh..." Not able to think of anything to say, she shoved a bite of eggs into her mouth, chewing carefully as she waited to see what else he would say, trying to not be distracted by his naked chest.

"I might've spent the last eight months thinking of you as a nice, grandmotherly teacher, but as soon as I saw you in the classroom, I was a goner. I was attracted to you when I saw you in those ridiculous coveralls in the hardware store, mumbling to yourself with your arms full of a crazy-ass assortment of stuff. I didn't have a clue you were the teacher who'd been writing to me. But you are the same sweet, funny, smart teacher that I had grown to care about, and discovering you were a beautiful, eligible woman made me start thinking that our pen pal friendship could be a lot more. But I just wasn't in the right headspace."

She cocked her head to the side, staying silent, curious for what he was going to say yet agonizing because she could see from his furrowed brow how difficult this was for him. Reaching across the table, she placed her hand on his arm.

"No man wants to come to a woman as unemployed with an uncertain future. I was excited to spend time with you, and being in your cottage, seeing what you're learning to do, I started having thoughts that went beyond just admiration. But I'd spent the last couple of months feeling sorry for myself, hating that I felt that way, and not being able to figure out what to do about it. I'd come home and spent time with my grandfather, helping him around the house, then I come here and discover that you've done much of the same type of things with no background and learning from YouTube videos. And while your method might have a bit of madness to it, I can't deny that you're getting some things done on top of working full time. I guess I just choked... felt like I had nothing to offer you other than a has-been soldier."

"Oh, John, I never wanted you to feel that way."

His fingers linked with hers as he ducked his head so that she was staring directly into his gaze. "Lucy, I know that. It was all on me. You're nothing but sunshine and light, and I felt nothing but dark anger and frustration."

"And the job is what makes it different now? Because you're more than just a job. That's only part of who you are."

He leaned back, his lips thinned as he pressed them together. She hoped he wouldn't shut her out but needed to know if he was ready for something or was going to keep running hot and cold.

"Does it sound like I'm some kind of alpha loser if I said yes?"

Unable to swallow the chortle that flew from her lips, she just shook her head. "What are you talking about? Alpha loser?"

His lips curved before he sighed. "For a long time, I was just the job. I had a career where I had to be in charge, a decision-maker, fast on my feet, and quick of mind. If not, people died. Yes, there was adrenaline and we lived off that kind of life. Hell, there are women who hang around military bases, attracted to being with that kind of man."

Brows lifted, she blinked. "Wow... um... okay, just wow."

His fingers squeezed on hers. "Babe, that was long in my past. Maybe my early twenties were spent not so discriminating in my partners, but I swear, those days have been long gone. For years now, I've only been with a few women, all ones I liked and respected, but in the end, knew they weren't for me."

She leaned in, kissing him lightly. "It's okay, John, you don't have to explain. It's not like I'm coming to you a blushing virgin... although I admit my list is probably significantly shorter than yours."

A growl left his lips and his brow lowered. "Okay... sex partner confessions have now been laid on the table, not to be brought up again."

She laughed, settling back in her chair. "Go on, keep talking."

"Anyway, I loved finding out more about you, but I was struggling with who I was outside of the Army Special Forces. Who I was outside the team. A man without a mission. Essentially, a man without a job. And sitting here in your house, I felt like I had nothing to bring to a new relationship."

"And you do now?"

"It might seem crazy to you considering I haven't even officially started work, but when you called, you needed me, and I would have done anything to make sure you were safe. Not because I was a soldier, but you needed *me*. And the job just means that I'll be employed in something that I'm good at, something that I'm proud of." His free hand drifted up to the scar near his eye but he held her gaze. "And that I can do the job regardless of this."

"You were always a hero to me." His intense gaze hit her, and she squeezed his hand, wanting him to take the words deep inside. "But now you're *my* hero."

"Damn, woman," he growled, tugging at her hand and pulling her from the chair.

She landed in his lap, his arms banding tightly around her as his lips met hers. Breakfast forgotten, they kissed, wet and wild. Noses bumped, teeth clashed, tongues tangled. Her fingers clenched his shoulders, and his hands held her cheeks.

She gave herself over to his kiss, intoxicated with the sensation of the zinging between her lips and core, her sex clenching with need. She mumbled against his lips, "Now."

He groaned. "I wanted to take you out—"

She separated, leaning back slightly. "John, we've known each other for the past eight months, even if you thought I was a little old lady. We've had dinner here. You've seen my house and my projects and managed to not insult what I'm attempting to do. You were the person I called when I was afraid. You came to rescue me. We spent hours talking, finding out about each other, learning more and more. We've spent the night together in the same bed. John, we don't need another date to know what we feel is real—*umph*!"

Her words were stolen as his lips landed on hers again. This time, the kiss flamed hot and wild instantly, setting her body on fire. Kissing finesse flew out the window as noses bumped and teeth met in an effort to devour each other. His groan set her blood on fire and she shifted to straddle his lap, now able to press her core against his impressive cock.

He stood and set her ass onto the table, leaning over her as he dragged his mouth from her lips down her chest, trailing kisses over the swell of flesh at the top of her T-shirt before grabbing the material with his teeth and pulling it down. Her fingers clutched his biceps as he latched onto a nipple, sucking it deeply into his mouth.

Electricity crackled about the room, and she grabbed the waistband of his jeans, wanting them off. "Naked," she managed to mumble.

He jerked away, and she groaned at the loss of his talented mouth on her breasts.

"No. Not like this," he declared.

She groaned even louder this time, ready to pin his body to hers and not let go. "John, please, I—"

"I don't mean 'no' to this or 'no' to now. But I'm not taking you for the first time on the kitchen table which I have no idea if it will hold our weight. Babe, our first time is going to be in your bed. Not only do you deserve that comfort, but I can also be reasonably sure we won't end up in a pile of splintered wood in the middle of the floor."

She burst out laughing as she was lifted and wrapped her legs around his waist and her arms around his neck, holding on as he stalked toward her bedroom.

She was prepared to be tossed onto the bed but

discovered quickly that John was in the mood to go gentle. He slowly lay her back onto the mattress, his hands gliding down her stomach and his fingers grasping the bottom of her shirt. As he pulled it upward, she lifted her arms over her head, giving him room to slide the material completely off. He tossed it to the side but her eyes never left his, loving the way his gaze settled on her breasts.

He bent over her, his tongue darting out to lick each swollen bud before kissing over her stomach, eliciting squirming tickle-giggles from her. Grinning, he snagged her sleep shorts and panties. Peeling them off with deliberation, his gaze followed his hands, his eyes flaring with each exposed inch. Now, completely exposed to his perusal, she felt worshiped, not exposed. Wanting him naked as well, he halted any words coming from her lips as he knelt on the floor, shouldered her knees apart, and settled between her thighs, his fingers parting her folds and his tongue diving into her sex.

Gasping at the sensation shooting between her core and her nipples, she grabbed the sheets, fisting them as she threw her head back. Her knees wanted to close, not to force him away but to ease the friction that was building, but his wide shoulders between her legs and one of his hands pressing down on her belly held her in place as he continued his delicious torture.

"God, John… I…" She had no more time to try to find words to describe what was happening because the moment his lips sucked her clit as he slid fingers deep into her channel, she cried out nonsensical utterances as her orgasm rushed over her. Stars pierced the blackness behind her closed eyes and her whole body shivered before her legs fell open, her ability to move now decimated.

When the quivering finally subsided, she managed to lift her head, open her eyes, and stare at a sight she never wanted to forget: John, his lips moist from her orgasm curving into a smile as his dark eyes held her gaze.

16

John stared at the beautiful woman lying in front of him, her taste on his tongue, her scent filling the air, a twinkle in her eyes, and a smile on her face. *Christ, almighty... she's everything.* As soon as that thought hit, it also struck him that he'd never in his thirty-four years ever felt that way about a woman.

He stood slowly and bent over her luscious body, kissing her lightly, allowing her to taste herself on his lips. The tiny moan that came from the depths of her reverberated through him, making his cock harder than it had been, and he'd never felt it so hard in his life. Standing straight again, he jerked his jeans down his legs, pulling his boxers off at the same time, freeing his cock.

She planted her elbows on the mattress and leaned up on her forearms, her eyes staring at his erection before lifting back to his face, the smile still on her lips.

She was right—they didn't need any longer to know what they felt was real.

He grabbed a condom from his wallet and ripped the foil open, rolling it over his cock before he crawled onto the bed. She had scooted upward so her whole body was on the mattress, her legs still open and her sex flush and ready as he planted his knees between her thighs. Placing the tip at her entrance, he held his weight off her chest but leaned down enough to glide his nose over hers. "Baby, you need to know what this is."

"John, I assure you I know what we're about to do," she whispered in return.

"Oh, no… I mean you really need to *know* what this is." He lifted his head to see the crinkle between her brows. "This is us. You and me. The start of something that I want to hold on to. Not just take what's here in front of us but build into everything we can… to become *us*. Do you understand?"

She blinked rapidly, moisture gathering in her eyes as she nodded. "Yes. I want that. I want you. Not just now but for as many tomorrows as you'll give me."

He grinned as he barely slid the tip of his cock into her sex. "Then plan on as many tomorrows as you can have, Lucy." With that, in one swift movement he plunged all the way, balls deep.

Her gasp sounded out, her fingers digging into his shoulders as her heels dug into his ass. The feel of her tight sex like a glove on his cock nearly made him come like an untried adolescent, but he halted his movements. "You okay?"

"Yes, God, just keep moving!"

Smirking, he was thrilled to follow her command. He continued to piston his hips, alternating his movements with slow, deliberate thrusts and hard, fast plunges. Her breasts bounced with the movements. Leaning over her chest, he sucked a rosy nipple into his mouth, her fingernails digging into his shoulders in a way that he knew he'd have little crescent marks. *Marked by her.* The slight sting made his erection swell even more, and he let her breast go with a pop. Shifting his weight to one hand, he slid his other to her mound, his thumb pressing on her clit.

He knew the second she flew apart, her thighs squeezing his waist, her inner walls squeezing his cock. Her head pressed back into the pillow. A flush ran from her breasts upward over her face as she cried out her orgasm, creating the most beautiful sight he'd ever seen in his life. Not wanting to hold back as his balls tightened and his lower spine burned, he lifted his head, felt the muscles in his neck cord, and his release rushed from his body. Barely able to drag oxygen into his lungs as his thrusts slowed until every drop was given, he fell forward, managing to land only partially on top of her, cushioned by her soft body.

The '*oof*' that fled her lips registered, and he forced his body to roll to the side while he banded his arms around her, dragging her with him so that they lay facing each other. Shifting his leg so that his thigh moved between hers, they stayed perfectly aligned, pressed together from chest to hip.

With his lips against her forehead, neither spoke for several minutes while their heart poundings slowed but still beat together. Finally, she leaned her head back, catching and holding his gaze, and grinned.

"Are you good, baby?" he asked, tucking a wild, wayward strand of hair behind her ear.

Still smiling, she nodded. "I'm perfect."

"Yeah, you are. Absolutely fuckin' perfect."

She must've liked his answer because she clutched his jaws, applied a little pressure to bring him closer which he didn't fight at all, and kissed him. And as soon as they recuperated, they started round two, not leaving her bed until finally dressing and running out for dinner.

John glanced at the GPS, turning onto the lane that cut through the thick evergreen forest that encroached upon the side of the road. While the Lighthouse Security Investigations headquarters were not secret, they also were not easy to find unless specific directions had been given. With his professional and practiced eye, he drove up to the security gate and could tell it was state-of-the-art, much more secure than the average person would ever realize. He looked directly toward the camera, knowing someone on the other end would be evaluating, deciding to let him in. The military-grade gate engaged, swinging open, allowing him to enter.

Continuing down the lane, the forests eventually fell away and an expanse of lush, green grass led to a lighthouse and a white house with a red roof at its base. The rocky cliff coast was just behind, dropping to the Atlantic Ocean below. His foot released the accelerator, allowing his gaze to take in the breathtaking scenery in front of him. *Damn.* No stranger to the beauty of Maine, he had to admit this particular view encapsulated the best of everything. Forest. Meadow. Rocky coast. Ocean. Lighthouse.

As he continued forward to park near the other vehicles, nerves hit his stomach, an emotion he was not used to. He had run forward toward missions for years and knew with his familiar team and careful planning exactly what his duty was. This was different. This group had been together for a while, at least most of them. He'd joined the Army at the age of eighteen, and for sixteen years it was the only job he had. Now he was the newbie. The one who was going to have to start out to prove himself.

True to Mace's word, he'd received paperwork through an online, secure channel the day before. He'd completed it, sending it back. Now all that was left was for him to walk through the door.

Climbing from his vehicle, he breathed deeply, the crisp, salty air of the spring morning filling his lungs. He walked to the house, following the instructions that had been given, and knocked on the door. It was flung open almost by the time he dropped his hand.

"You found us, good. Good. Come on in, John." Horace, grinning widely, reached his hand out for a shake.

He stepped inside the house, immediately entering a large kitchen. A woman was standing at the counter, her gray hair tidy, a grandmotherly appearance about her, and yet as soon as her steely eyes landed on him he knew he was being evaluated. And with the expression on her face, he hoped he met with her approval.

Horace clapped a hand on John's shoulder and waved toward the woman. "I'd like you to meet my better half. This is my wife, Marge."

He stepped forward, shaking her hand. "It's a pleasure to meet you, Mrs. Tiddle."

She offered a firm handshake, her sharp eyes taking him in before her lips curved slightly. "Just call me Marge. I've heard a lot about you already, John. Bray sings your praises, and Mace is excited to have you on board. From what I understand, your actions this weekend speak highly for you. You'll find that around here that kind of selfless dedication goes a long way— even more than your military background."

Her words surprised him, and unable to think of a response, he simply nodded. "Thank you."

"Horace and I take care of the grounds and the buildings of LSI. I dare say you've probably heard that we take care of the Keepers as well." A wide smile finally broke out on her face as though she'd come to a conclusion. "Welcome aboard."

"I'm glad to be here," he assured. A sound from the back hall captured his attention, and he swung his head around to see Mace walking into the kitchen.

Shaking hands, Mace instructed, "Follow me, John. I'll take you to the others and go through the security for you. Sylvie got your paperwork, we've already done an initial security check and clearance that extends the one you had with the Army, and your signed nondisclosure is in place. Before you leave, Sylvie will have you sign a few things. Mostly personnel and tax forms. Once you're completely in her system, our security will add your information so that you won't need to be escorted to get to the main room."

Multiple questions flew through his mind, but he kept his mouth shut and his eyes open— one of the early lessons he learned in boot camp many years ago, and it had always served him well.

They moved through the house, his gaze taking in the space, noting it appeared to be just like any other house. Mace, who he figured didn't miss much— including his perusal—said, "I grew up near here, and when I had the opportunity, I bought the decommissioned lighthouse and keeper's house. As a child, I'd discovered some of the caverns that run underneath, many used by smugglers in centuries past. Sylvie and I live with our son on the property that I grew up in, my grandfather's house."

They walked down a back hall toward the base of the lighthouse. He looked up at the concrete, spiral stairs that led up to the top.

"It's a great view. We'll go up there before you leave."

He observed with keen interest as Mace turned to the opposite wall and flipped open a hidden panel. Tapping in a security code, he stood while a retina scan occurred, then placed his hand on a finger scanner. A door swung open, and Mace entered, inviting John to step in with him. Discovering they were in an elevator, he watched again as Mace tapped in another security code and they began their descent. At the bottom, the door swung open and they entered another hallway, stopping at a heavy metal door. Mace went through the motions of the security systems again.

It appeared this was the final door as they stepped through, entering a cavernous room. The walls and ceilings were reinforced with what appeared to be steel beams and panels. The concrete floor was smooth and solid but retained the look of the original cave. Recognizing the room was sealed and protected, there were two walls filled with computer equipment and stations with several men manning the keyboards. Other computer equipment filled the back wall, and the fourth wall held large screens with multiple images flashing upon them. Various doors opened from the large room, but his attention focused on the people in the room, all eyes turned his way.

Tamping down his nerves, he was glad he'd met many of them before and breathed a little easier when he saw that their faces all held smiles. He had no problem admitting it was going to be a helluva lot easier to start a new job with a genuine welcome as opposed to a group of competitive strangers.

He recognized Babs sitting at a desk next to another one where a beautiful woman had just stood and was walking toward him with her hand extended. Mace's taciturn expression warmed as he smiled, reaching over to wrap his arm around her shoulders.

"John, meet my wife and LSI's office manager, Sylvie."

Sylvie smiled, shaking his hand. "It's wonderful to finally meet you, John. Welcome to LSI."

"It's a pleasure, ma'am. I understand you have some forms for me."

"I'm Sylvie, please. And yes, after you're finished here, just stop by my desk, and I'll make sure we have everything taken care of."

He nodded his acquiescence and turned to greet Babs, laughing as she called out, "Heard your Lucy thinks fast under pressure."

My Lucy. Keeping his expression neutral, he nodded. "That she does."

"Good," Babs quipped. "That just proves she's got what it takes."

With his head cocked slightly to the side, he wondered what she meant but didn't ask.

Shaking her head while still laughing, she said, "You'll find out what I mean."

Before he had a chance to decipher Babs' cryptic comments, Mace turned him toward the others. They walked around the room and he was introduced to the Keepers he hadn't met and reintroduced to Drew, Tate, Clay, Josh, and Walker. As Mace continued, John gained a quick overview of what they were working on.

"We run security, specializing in systems that go way beyond typical security. We don't take on positions as bodyguards, although we have accepted security escort contracts for certain clients, namely government agencies. Our systems are used by government officials, foreign dignitaries, a few celebrities but not many of those. They tend to be a pain in the ass, and that's not worth our time. There are lots of other security agencies that take care of celebrities. Mostly our monitors are only for those we deem necessary. The rest we contract out to other security agencies for constant monitoring. Our investigations include being called in by the FBI, government contracts, needs of other law enforcement, even rescues, just to name a few."

John took in everything Mace was saying, nerves now being replaced by excitement. "I was impressed the first time I heard about LSI, but after seeing it and meeting your staff, I have to say I'm blown away by what you've done here."

Mace nodded, motioning him to sit at the large round table near the center of the room. Seated to Mace's left, others filled in, tablets in front of them.

"What I want to do now is bring you up to speed on the Minotaurs. We've been working with the Canadians and the U.S. Department of Justice's Organized Crime Drug Enforcement Task Force to help investigate drug trafficking between the United States and Canada, particularly with the biker gangs. You already know that the Minotaurs had been taken in and are working with the Hell's Angels. With the information you called in, what you don't know yet is that James Kinder, aka Griz, rose to a high level with one of the Montana chapters of the Hell's Angels, then moved to Canada to assist with the takeovers of biker gangs there. He now runs between Maine and Michigan and into Quebec and Ontario as a Minotaur. Depending on where he is, he can wear cuts of both."

Every word that Mace said brought a deeper level of fear into John's heart at the thought of Lucy not only being in the presence of Griz but now on his radar. He went back over everything that Lucy had told him, now more than ever pleased with her level of detail, something the others mentioned as well.

"Chances are Griz has no reason to give Lucy a second thought, but I want to have security on her place anyway."

"She'll have no problem with that," John said. "While she kept a cool head, the bikers scared her, especially Griz."

Bray looked over from his side of the table. "What about her friend? Paula?"

"Hardly a friend anymore, I think. Lucy won't be taking any more trips or spending time with her, but they do work in the same building. It's going to be impossible for her to not have some dealings with Paula."

The others around the table nodded, but it was clear from their tight jaws and lips pressed together that they would prefer Lucy never have to be around Paula at all.

"Let's put Paula's place in our sights also," suggested Drew. "We know Griz has been in this area. If he met with her in Canada, then it's not too far-fetched to think that he won't continue to have contact with her."

Mace nodded, rubbing his chin. John hesitated, not knowing his place amongst them, something Mace picked up on almost immediately.

"John, if you've got something to say, say it. You're one of us now. We throw out ideas, bounce things off each other. There's no hierarchy here."

"Other than everyone is subservient to me and Sylvie," Babs shouted out from her desk, drawing laughter from everyone, the loudest coming from her husband, Drew.

John grinned, then sobered as he looked at the others. "I just can't figure Paula out. Nothing seemed to fit with her. A teacher. A friend to Lucy, although I'm not sure how close they are. I haven't had the resources to check her or her background out, but Lucy is a well-grounded, smart person and says she's never had red flags about Paula's behavior other than being a flirt and has no fear. On top of that, she hardly seems like the type of person Griz would hang around. It just doesn't add up."

Mace looked over at Josh. "Do a background workup on Paula. Finances, history, family. Let's find out what's going on." Turning to Clay, he said, "You and Levi get in contact with the FBI and our liaison with the Drug Task Force. Let them know what we have and what we're looking at."

As orders were being given, John's mind was spinning. A new job, one where he started out respected and on par with the others. A chance to take his sixteen years in the Army, most of those as Special Forces, and use the talents and skills he'd learned. And Lucy... Not only was she now planted fully in his life but the Keepers were working to ensure her safety.

The next hours were spent shadowing several of the Keepers as they worked at their individual stations and spending time researching what he could learn about the Minotaurs. The more he learned, the more he breathed a sigh of relief that Lucy had been able to escape their notice.

Lunch was often on their own, but today they all moved upstairs to the large dining room where Marge had fixed a huge sandwich buffet for them.

During the afternoon, he learned about the security cameras they would put in place around Lucy's house.

By the end of the day, Mace kept his promise and the two of them climbed the circular stairs to the top of the lighthouse. John grinned as they made their way past the lamps and looked out over the sparkling water and crashing waves. He was hard-pressed to think of a more impressive sight.

"I bring everyone up here when they are taken on as a Keeper," Mace said, the two men standing at the rail side by side. "It's a perfect opportunity to remind them what we're doing. The old lighthouses were maintained by ordinary men and women who were heroes as they went about their business keeping the ships and sailors safe. That's what we do. We won't get the glory. Our cases solved will be claimed by other law enforcement or not claimed at all. But we work every day knowing that our jobs keep others safe."

"I understand." The view in front of him was breathtaking and John thought how much he'd like to bring Lucy to the top of the lighthouse. Turning to Mace, he asked, "What did Babs mean when she mentioned Lucy this morning?"

Chuckling, Mace dropped his chin and stared at his boots for a moment before swinging his gaze back to John. "So far, every one of the keepers who's married or engaged has met their significant other on a mission. It's become evident to all of us that it takes a very special kind of person to be able to handle being with a Keeper. From everything you've said, Lucy fits that description."

He'd never met the other women, but if they were as brave and special as Lucy, he had no doubt that she'd fit in.

Mace stepped back from the rail and turned toward him. "Remember, John, you're now a Keeper. You're not defined by the injury that caused you to leave the Army. You're defined by what's inside of you."

Sucking in a deep breath of clean, ocean air, John nodded. "Thank you for the opportunity, Mace. I won't let you down."

Clapping him on the shoulder, Mace grinned. "I know you won't. If I thought for one second you would, you wouldn't be standing here with me now."

17

"Hey, Paula. I'm glad you got home okay." Lucy made sure her smile was bright, and her voice gave no evidence of ire. John was at LSI for his first day, but the day before they'd talked about how she should play her interaction when she saw Paula at school. John had advised her that until he had a chance to talk to the others, it would be best to not let Paula know that she'd seen anything untoward. She'd taken a drama class in high school and figured it was time to put some of those acting skills to work.

Paula's nerves were written in her expression and her lips trembled slightly as she smiled, her eyes darting to the side before moving back to Lucy's.

Before giving Paula a chance to say anything, Lucy continued. "I hope you got my text. It was nice of you to offer me the hotel room but I really just wanted to get home. I promised my parents that I'd be at their place yesterday and didn't want to disappoint them."

"Oh... uh... yeah. I'm sorry. I shouldn't have changed plans on you." Paula's lips attempted to curve upward but her smile was forced. "So, you got a ride?"

"Yes, I called a friend who came to get me."

"Wow, that was a long way for someone to come," Paula muttered, her fingers fiddling with the strap of her school bag.

No shit... "Oh, they didn't mind. I hung around the festival some more, ate a ton of food that probably all ended up on my hips," she said with a laugh and a toss of her hand. "I bought a few things at the vendors, and by the time the bands were over, my friend was there. We had a good time talking on the way home, and then I was able to be with my parents yesterday."

"Good, good." Paula's voice was stronger, her smile a little wider.

"So, did you and Griz have a good time? I figured when you got my message and knew I wasn't using the room you might have gone back there."

"Yeah, it was great. Um... I drank too much, of course. That's why I need to apologize to you. I feel like I was such a bitch and didn't mean to be. But... yeah, we went to the hotel. I let them know that you weren't going to be there, so we figured we might as well use the room."

Lucy watched as Paula continued to force a smile, unable to keep the slight tremor from her lips. The bell rang, and Lucy grabbed her items from the teacher's workroom. "My class is heading to physical education with Mrs. Farthingale, but I've got to head back to my room to finish some plans. I'll talk to you later."

Paula nodded, her head moving in jerks. Lucy turned and left the room, her anger ratcheting up with each step. While her friendship with Paula was only a couple of years old, she'd thought she knew her. Paula tended to drink more than Lucy, who never liked to lose control. Paula also had no problem with one-night stands, while Lucy, who had no problem with her sexuality, preferred sleeping with someone that she'd gotten to know. But she'd never known Paula to take drugs, have anything to do with drugs, be around drugs, and certainly not be around someone who was known to sell drugs.

Sure, Paula sometimes likes the occasional bad boy, but Griz? The Paula she'd gotten to know would've never put her in danger. Now, she wondered if she'd ever really known Paula or if something had happened to make her change. Rubbing her forehead as she entered her classroom, she wished she could make all the conflicting thoughts go away.

Glancing at the clock, she sighed in relief knowing she had thirty minutes to go before her students came back into the classroom. Sitting at her desk, she'd just pulled out her plan book when her phone vibrated. Grabbing it out of her purse, she smiled as John's name appeared on the screen.

"Hey, how on earth did you know I needed to hear your voice?"

"What's up, babe?"

"Oh, nothing. I just had my first interaction with Paula. But I don't want to talk about her. Tell me how work is going, that is if you can talk about anything without having to kill me."

He chuckled, and the sound of his mirth eased her frustration. "I can't talk about specifics, but I can tell you that it's been phenomenal. I feel like I've been given a second lease on life."

His words warmed her heart and she breathed a sigh of relief. "Oh, John, I'm so glad! That makes me happy. In fact, that's been the best thing I've heard all day."

"Yep. Good people. Good place. Good work."

"Then you'll fit right in."

"Damn, babe, you're good for my ego."

She laughed, enjoying the lighthearted sound of his mirth as well.

"Okay, Lucy. Now, tell me what happened with Paula."

"Don't worry, it was fine. I didn't see her this morning but ran into her in the teacher's workroom. I did exactly as we decided. A happy smile, happy voice. I pretended that all was well, told her I had not even gone to the hotel, and I just hung around at the festival until a friend came to pick me up."

"Think she believed you?"

"Absolutely. I think she was so nervous that I was going to get up in her face, so she was just thrilled that I acted like nothing was wrong. She did seem surprised that a friend would come that far to get me but I just said they didn't mind."

"Well, that part was no lie."

His deep voice rumbled over the airwaves, moving inside of her. A smile curved her lips and she leaned back in her chair, more relaxed. "Have I told you how sweet you are, John Roster?"

"I think you have, babe. Have I told you how beautiful you are, Lucy Carrington?"

A bark of laughter erupted, and she sighed. "Thank you. I was so keyed up after talking to Paula, and in just a few minutes you've already made me feel so much better."

"Well, I hope the next thing I tell you doesn't take you out of your good mood."

Bolting upright in her chair, she said, "Oh, no. Tell me what?"

"I went over everything with my coworkers. They have things they're working on which I won't go into with you, but they also feel like it would be prudent for us to have some eyes on your house."

Scrunching her nose, she shook her head slightly. "Eyes on my house. What does that mean?"

"Security, babe. A couple of cameras on your front and back entrances, just to make sure that no one is trying to get to you."

She said nothing as she nibbled on her bottom lip, her mind racing. "Okay. That doesn't sound too obtrusive. I'm assuming you agree?"

"Yes, absolutely. To be honest, I'm so new to what LSI does that I'd be willing to put my trust in any decision they came up with. In this case, I agree that it's the right thing to do."

Sighing heavily, she said, "Okay, then they can do whatever they need to do. Although, let me just go on

the record as saying that I prefer you being there as my
up close, personal security."

"Damn, girl, you've got to cut that out. I'm just
finishing up my day here, and I don't want to walk back
into the room with a hard-on."

Laughter rang out again, but before she had a chance
to say anything else, he jumped in with another
surprise.

"I've barely seen Gramps in the past two days but I
gave him a quick rundown of what was going on. I need
to have dinner with him tonight, and he wants to meet
you. So, I'm going to pick you up as soon as I get off and
bring you back to his house so we can all have dinner
together."

"Whoa, seriously? Are you sure? I mean, if you just
want to have dinner with your Gramps, that's fine."

"Of course, I'm sure. We decided to see where we're
going in this relationship, and part of being together is
going to be involved with each other's families. And
believe me, when Gramps gets his mind set on something, it's best to go along with it. He wants you at the
dinner table tonight."

"Well, alrighty then. Looks like I'll be having dinner
with the Roster men. And by the way, I had already
planned on inviting you and your Gramps to my family's Memorial Day picnic. You just happened to jump
the gun on meeting the families, but I call dibs on
getting everyone together."

"Sounds good, babe. Be careful and avoid Paula if
you can. I'll pick you up at your place as soon as I get off
work."

Disconnecting, she leaned back in her chair again, her heart much lighter with thoughts of John filling her mind. Then, due to the idea that she was going to have to have cameras on her house because of her former friend's stupidity, she almost lost her good mood again. Pushing that to the side, she decided to spend her next few minutes planning what to take to dinner as she waited for her class to return.

Lucy waited on the front porch, her hands full. She'd baked a strawberry crumble pie, glad that she had fresh strawberries from the farmer's market and a frozen pie crust in her freezer. Her gaze stayed on the drive, anxious for John to arrive. She'd only said goodbye to him yesterday, but it would be the first time they would be around someone else since they had become a couple.

She shifted the pie to one hand so she could smooth her skirt with the other. Deciding what to wear had taken almost as long as deciding what to bake. Meeting his only relative, the man who'd helped raise him, was a big deal. Too dressy would seem like overkill considering John had described his grandfather as a practical man, but then jeans would feel like she didn't care to make a good impression. She'd finally decided on a casual skirt that fell to her calves, a T-shirt with lace at the top and little cap sleeves, and sandals.

The rumble of a large vehicle had her gaze jump back to the lane, and seeing his smile through the windshield of the SUV eased her nerves. She hurried down her front steps, tripping at the bottom on a loose nail then righting herself quickly before she lost control of the pie. He jumped down from behind the wheel, hustling toward her.

"Are you okay?" He took the pie plate from her hands, his gaze glancing back at the steps.

"Oh, yes. Just a loose nail I keep forgetting to hammer in all the way."

He wrapped his arm around her shoulders and guided her toward the passenger side where he assisted her up into the seat, handing her the pie once she was buckled. "The boards in the steps should be screwed in. That would make them more secure."

She scrunched her nose and sighed. "Oh. Well, I've just replaced a few of the boards, but I need to work on the whole thing. I suppose I need to add that to my list of things to get done."

His deep chuckle filled the air. "How long is that list now?"

"Hmph." Grousing, she play-slapped him on the arm.

It only took fifteen minutes to drive to Gramps' house, and he spent most of that time warning her about his grandfather. "I don't want you to be put off by him, but he's a bit of a curmudgeon." Sliding his hand around the back of his neck, he squeezed. "Actually, he's a lot of a curmudgeon."

"It'll be fine," she assured.

"I just don't want you to be offended by anything he says. He's pretty blunt but harmless. He takes care of himself but his arthritis makes it a little more difficult."

She twisted and placed her hand on his leg. "John, stop worrying. It'll be fine." She leaned forward in her seat as they turned off the main road, driving through thick trees. At the end was a clearing, a grey-clapboard house coming into sight. "Oh, I love it," she enthused.

He swung his head to the side as he parked next to the house. "Only you would see an old house that needs more repairs—and that's after I've spent a couple of weeks doing lots of repairs—and say that you love it."

"Are you determined to get on my bad side before we go inside?"

He leaned over the console, his hand on the back of her head, and pulled her gently toward him, landing a kiss on her lips. She immediately melted, and it hit her that she might never stay irritated at him as long as he kissed her that way. But that was a secret she was willing to keep this early in their relationship.

Separating the barest inch, he held her gaze. "I never want to get on your bad side, and to be honest, I love that you love old houses."

Her smile widened as he let her go. He rounded the vehicle and assisted her down as she carefully maintained hold of the pie. Stepping inside the kitchen, she sniffed in appreciation at the scents coming from the stove. An older man turned, his gaze taking her in before the creases deepened as he smiled. His hair was white, the top sparse but the sides combed neatly. His pants were a little baggy but clean and his white shirt was pressed. After everything John had told her, she could tell he'd made an effort, and she was glad she'd chosen to wear a skirt. She smiled as he walked toward her.

"You must be Lucy." His voice was gravelly but warm.

"Yes, Mr. Roster. Thank you for having me."

"Call me Gramps. Nobody's formal around here."

"Okay, I will. And I brought a strawberry crumble pie for dessert. I hope that's okay."

"Never knew a man to turn down a pretty girl with dessert in her hands." He winked, and she caught sight of John rolling his eyes.

"Gramps, are you flirting with my girl?"

"Never knew an old man to *not* flirt with a pretty girl with dessert in her hands."

Lucy laughed as she set the pie on the counter. She looked around at the kitchen; clean, but it hadn't been updated in years, and she wondered how different it would have been when John's grandmother was alive.

"Lucy commented on how much she loved the house when we drove up," John said.

"It's old. 'Bout the best you can say for it." Gramps moved slowly back to the stove. "John, take the fish pie out of the oven."

John moved to handle the hot dish, placing it on a worn potholder sitting in the middle of the table. Three places were already set, and she glanced over to see a pitcher of iced tea on the counter. "Would you like me to pour?"

"Be fine, Lucy," Gramps said. "Then sit yourself down, and we'll eat. No ceremony here, so make yourself at home."

Soon, they were at the table and she moaned in appreciation at her first bite. "It's been a while since I've had fish pie, and this is delicious."

Gramps grinned. "My wife's recipe. I don't do fancy cooking, but she was a good cook. Whenever we had company, she'd make her Maine Haddock Pie. Figured John bringing home a girl was reason enough to celebrate."

"Well, I'm honored."

The conversation was easy as Gramps asked her about teaching and then asked John about his first day at work. She could tell John was fluffing his answers, but Gramps didn't seem to care that John had to keep most of what he'd be doing a secret.

She served the pie and was thrilled when Gramps pulled vanilla ice cream from the freezer. Making a pot of coffee which they took to the living room, Gramps settled into an old recliner while she and John sat together on the sofa.

"I hear you're working on your house," Gramps said.

"Yes. I bought an old house that needed a lot of love. My parents despaired since I knew nothing about repairs. But I've learned as I go. I contracted out the electrical work and larger plumbing work, but I've updated the kitchen and the master bathroom, doing a lot of the work myself."

"What's this youbie tubie thing John said you were learning from?"

Her eyes widened, not understanding, and she shot John a questioning look.

John laughed, saying, "He means YouTube."

"Oh," she laughed as well, blushing. "It's a... um... well, it's a place on the internet where people can post all kinds of videos. And some of them show you how to do things. So, I just search for whatever I'm working on, like *how to tile a kitchen backsplash* and a bunch of videos will pop up on my computer to show me how to do it. Some are better than others, so I look for the ones for beginners."

Gramps' fork had halted on its way to his mouth, his bushy eyebrows raised. "Hmph. In my day, we learned by what our dads or granddads taught us."

"I'm sure my dad would show me, but then he has a penchant for taking over. But on my own, I've done a lot, including replacing some boards in the porch, which I now know from John that I needed to have used screws instead of nails, so I'll do those over."

"Seems to me if John thinks there's a better way to do something, he should offer to do it himself."

She blinked in surprise, ready to defend John, but he burst out laughing next to her. "Gramps, I planned on helping her out but needed to have a chance to offer in a way that didn't make it seem like I was taking over. Lucy is determined to take care of her house herself. You've jumped the gun on me."

She smiled at John as his arm around her shoulder pulled her closer. "You don't have to offer to help—"

"Honey, I was going to but knew I needed to find a way to do it so you'd accept my help."

Biting her lip, she crinkled her nose. "I promise I won't get prickly. At least working with you will be fun.

When my brother helps, he gets annoying. I always have to remind him that it's *my* house!"

Gramps cackled as he sat back in his seat. "I like you, Lucy. You've got spunk. And anytime you get bored at your house, you come on over here and can tell John what to do with this old heap."

Turning her smile toward him, she nodded her agreement. "Thank you, Gramps. I might just do that!"

18

John took off his ball cap and wiped his brow. It was now the next Saturday, and while the day was not hot, the sun beamed down in a blue, cloudless sky. He'd knelt over Lucy's front porch, showing her how to use the cordless drill to screw in the wood screws to hold her porch boards more securely. When he'd come over that morning, he'd planned on doing it himself but soon learned that just like with her dad, while Lucy accepted his assistance, she wanted to learn.

"I'm always telling my students that we're never too old to learn new things. If I let you take over a house project, I know it would get done quicker, but I won't have learned anything."

It was hard to argue with her logic although it went against his nature to not want to jump in and do everything for her. But then, soon, with their conversation flowing and lighthearted banter, not to mention stolen kisses, he discovered that working on a project together had its advantages.

Dressed in her coveralls again, he now knew what her body looked like underneath and it was hard not to get *hard* just thinking of peeling them off. Dragging his focus off his dick and back to her, he caught her glancing up at the security camera in the corner of the porch that he, Bray, and Tate had installed a few days earlier.

She sucked in her lips before turning to him. "I haven't thought much about the security but it's a little weird knowing someone can see us."

"It's not monitored twenty-four-seven, but it gives us information in case someone does come snooping around."

Just like he'd discovered about most things with Lucy, she was easygoing and simply shrugged as she went back to her task. When the last screw was in place, they walked together over the porch, and he laughed as she squealed in delight at the secure boards with no nails left to trip on.

"Okay, babe, what's next?"

She wrapped her arms around his waist and beamed up at him. "We're going to have lunch first. Then we'll take a hike in the woods on my property, and I can show you my surprise."

It didn't take long for them to finish their sandwiches and chips, and he watched in curiosity as she grabbed a small tote, filling it with sunscreen, bug spray, and water bottles.

"How long are we going to be gone? That makes it look like we'll be hiking for miles."

Laughing, she shook her head. "It's not that big, but this will be part of my surprise."

Soon, she led him out the back door and onto a mulched path that led into the woods. Waving her hands with animation as they walked, she talked about the end of the school year coming. "We're having a Field Day and Party in two weeks. The kids wanted to know if you'd be able to come. I think they'd love to run races with you."

"Sounds good." His answer tripped lightly off his tongue, and it struck him that he meant what he said. It wasn't that long ago that the idea of spending time with a bunch of ten-year-olds would have held no appeal, hating that the reason he'd have time to do it was because he was out of the Army. But with a new job and Gramps and Lucy in his life, he found new things to be excited about. And he spent less and less time thinking about his vision.

They made their way over three acres, and just as he wondered how far back her property went, they came upon a wide expanse of water with a canoe tied to a tiny wooden dock.

Lucy whirled around and swung his arm with their connected hands. "See! My property backs to this tributary that leads to a bay that leads to the ocean!"

"Seriously?" He stared in surprise, then laughed as she continued to talk while giving a little hop.

"And this is my canoe! My brother bought it for us to use, and we're taking it out today. That's my surprise!"

Her eyes lit as she smiled up at him, sparkling as

much as the sunlight on the water. With fingers linked, he pulled her closer and dipped to take her lips. Pulling back regretfully, he mumbled, "Best surprise, babe."

The dock was sturdy, and he stepped into the canoe, lifting his hand to assist Lucy as she climbed in after him. Settled on either end, she placed her bag onto the floor, and they dipped their paddles into the water, gliding out over the surface.

It had been a while since he'd been on the water, and for a few seconds, he closed his eyes as he lifted his chin, allowing the sunlight to warm him deep inside. Hearing a splash, he opened his eyes to see Lucy looking to the side.

"There's fish jumping," she said, her voice now soft. "My dad said this summer would be a good time to go fishing. I haven't done that in a long time."

The last time he'd fished had been on a mission in South America and his team fished to eat, but he kept that tidbit to himself. Although, it didn't pass his notice that he could think about his team without the sharp ache inside his chest.

"Do you miss it?"

He jerked his head around to see her staring at him, her head cocked to the side. "Miss what?"

"The Special Forces? Your team? The missions?"

Surprised, he dropped his chin. *Shouldn't be surprised... not with Lucy.* Her perception was one of the things that drew him to her. Sighing, he lifted his head and smiled. "Yes and no. Yes, I'll always think fondly of those guys that were my brothers. And I want to keep up with them, something I haven't been good at doing since I got out. But I have a life now that's outside the service. And even though it's taken a while to get used to, I'm a hell of a lot luckier than so many others."

"I think the fact that you can now realize how lucky you are says a great deal about you."

Nodding slowly as his paddle dipped into the water, propelling them forward, he agreed. "I wasn't sure about coming home. I wasn't sure about my place here with Gramps. I didn't have a job. I didn't have friends. But now, Gramps and I might get in each other's way a little bit, but I think we're both glad I'm here. I can't believe I've got a job that suits me so well. And I never thought about having someone like you in my life."

The canoe rocked as she jerked her paddle upward and plopped it into the bottom near her seat. Without giving him a warning, she crawled forward over the seats, getting closer, a gleam in her eye.

He grinned widely as she crawled in between his legs, placing her hands on his thighs. "What have you got on your mind, babe?"

"While the scenery around us is gorgeous, what's filling my eyes is sitting right in front of me. Although no one else is around, what I'd like to do to you out here in the open is probably illegal."

Barking out laughter, he nodded. "I can definitely tell you that what I'd like to do to you out here in the open is absolutely illegal."

She leaned up, still balancing her weight with her hands on his thighs. Her lips landed on his, and they kissed, long, hard, and wet. His cock swelled, uncomfortable in his cargo shorts, sitting on the hard bench of the canoe. Holding the paddle with one hand, his other hand banded around her waist and pulled her close so that her breasts were plastered against his chest. Angling his head for better access, his tongue dove in, drowning in her taste.

He lost sense of time but was jolted when the canoe came to a sudden halt. They separated and looked around, seeing they had run into a small log across part of the tributary. Lifting his hand, he cupped her cheek. "I've loved your surprise, but what do you say about going back to your house and continuing what we've started?"

With her eyes still shining, her breath rasped in before she smiled. "I thought this was a good idea, but I like your idea better!"

They made short work of getting back to the dock and securing the canoe. Once it was tied off, he grabbed her hand and they raced through the woods toward her house. Rushing through the back door, she laughed, gasping for breath. "If your coworkers are watching, what will they think about us running into the house?"

He whirled around and lifted her onto the kitchen counter, stepping between her legs and nestling his erection next to her core. Her eyes darkened, and she bit her lip, breathing heavily.

"They'll see me with a gorgeous woman and think I'm the luckiest man alive."

Snapping out her hands to clutch his jaws, she pulled him in for another kiss. He gave her that play, then, picking her up off the counter, he carried her to her bedroom, only this time he didn't stop until he'd made it into her bathroom. With one arm still banded about her waist, he reached his free hand to the shower and turned on the faucet.

He lowered her feet to the floor slowly, allowing her body to glide down his. Keeping their fronts plastered together, his cock nestled snugly against her tummy. Ending the kiss just long enough for them to jerk their clothes off, they were naked in record time. He stepped inside the shower first so the water would hit his back, allowing her a chance to step in without getting pummeled directly in her face.

She slipped in after him and turned to face him, her gaze dropping over his body, snagging on his erection.

Taking her in, all curves and softness, his cock bobbed in anticipation. "Turn around," he ordered gently.

She tilted her head for a few seconds, then grinned and obeyed. Presented with her back, his gaze now traced down the slope of her spine and the gorgeous globes of her ass. He wanted to bend her over and take her from behind, but first, he wanted to take care of her. Grabbing her shampoo, he lathered her hair, dragging his fingers along her scalp, loving the little moans she made as she leaned her head back. Stepping to the side, he let the water wash away the suds before he repeated his actions with the bottle of conditioner that he discovered sitting on the shower shelf.

As soon as he finished, she turned around and her smile shot straight through him. She leaned forward, her breasts touching his chest as she snagged body wash from the shelf. Pouring some onto her palm, she rubbed her hands together before placing them flat on his chest and soothing them over the ridges of his pecs and shoulders before gliding down his abs. Stepping closer again, she let her hands move over his ass, gripping slightly before she shifted to his painfully swollen cock.

Unable to take any more of her ministrations without coming right there in the shower, he banded his arms around her and lifted. Growling as he backed her against the now-warm tile, he used his leverage to maintain her position as he bent and sucked a nipple deeply into his mouth. Her fingernails dug into the muscles of his shoulders as he moved between each breast, nipping and sucking. Sliding one hand between them, his thumb circled her clit as he inserted a finger into her channel. Working her body like a fine instrument, his onslaught was complete as she cried out, her sex vibrating against his finger.

Pulling his fingers out, he slid them into his mouth, sucking her essence as her wide eyes stayed pinned on him. Moving his hand to his cock, he placed the tip at her entrance, then halted. "Fuck, a condom."

"I'm clean. And I'm on the pill." She winced. "I know that's what every woman who's trying to trap a man probably says. We can stop and get a condom—"

"I'm clean, too. We were tested all the time in the service, and I haven't been with a woman in months. Hell, months and months if I'm honest. I trust you but it's your call, babe."

Her hands clutched his jaws, and she nodded, her smile curving her lips once again. "I trust you, too. With everything, about everything, I trust you."

Her words meant more to him than just where he placed his unsheathed cock. She trusted him to take care of her, and he wasn't about to squander that trust. He closed the distance as he angled his head and took her lips in a searing kiss. The water pounded them from the side, but all he could think of was the feel of her body yielding to his.

With his cock once again at her entrance, he thrust his hips, entering her quickly. His desire to take her hard and fast had faded with their vows, and he moved slowly, dragging his erection along her inner walls. The sensation of bare skin against bare skin was like a drug, one he never wanted to quit.

With only a few more thrusts, his balls tightened, and he knew he was close, but wanted to take care of her again. "Babe, are you close?"

"Yes," she barely gasped, her eyes squeezed tightly closed as she held on to his shoulders as though afraid if she let go he would disappear.

"Open your eyes. Look at me."

She immediately acquiesced, and he stared into her brown eyes, loving the sight of her coming again. She cried out his name as the flush moved from her full breasts up to her face, her nipples beading. Just as her inner muscles were squeezing his erection, his muscles tightened and he roared out his own release. With one hand under her ass and the other hand planted against the shower wall next to her head, he pumped slowly until every drop had been wrung from his body. He pressed his chest against hers, keeping her pinned against the wall as his cock slid out of her sex. Making sure to keep her steady, he lowered her until her feet were securely on the shower floor.

Uncertain either of their legs would hold them up, he was glad for the tiled, built-in bench in the corner. He flipped off the now-cooling water. Slumping onto the bench, he pulled her into his lap, their arms wrapped around each other as they steadied their heartbeats and their breathing.

"I knew I loved this shower when I reworked the bathroom." She grinned. "Maybe next time we can explore bathtub sex."

He barked out a laugh, and his arms flexed, squeezing her. "That's a deal, babe."

When they finally recovered, he assisted her out of the shower and onto the plush bath mat, loving the feel of her thick towels as they dried each other off. "I think Gramps has been using the same threadbare towels for years and years."

"There's not a lot of things I'll splurge on, but nice sheets and nice towels are a must for me." She walked naked into her room, his gaze following her every movement. She pulled on fresh underwear before wrapping up in a short, brightly colored kimono.

He dressed in the clothes he'd worn over, then stepped closer, reaching out with both hands and linking her fingers with his. Kissing her forehead, he kept his lips against her soft skin and asked, "What else is a must for you?"

She leaned back, her gaze hitting him, her dark eyes penetrating. Her lips curved ever so slightly, and she took a deep breath before letting it out slowly. "You."

Her single-word answer slammed into him, echoing exactly what he'd been feeling. His smile started from his chest and moved out, and he could only imagine how wide it was by the time it reached his face. Bending so that his lips were a whisper away from hers, he agreed. "Same for me, babe. *You* have become a must for me."

19

"She's clean, at least from the initial investigation."

John frowned at Josh's news. Sitting at the large round table in the LSI headquarters, he was already more comfortable in his new work setting. He looked forward to his first in-the-field assignment but having a job he was proud of as well as being with Gramps and now having Lucy in his life made being home worthwhile.

Now, focusing on Josh's pronouncement, he shook his head. "How can Paula be that squeaky clean?"

Josh chuckled, looking up from his computer screen. "Well, I didn't say squeaky. No priors. No arrests. A couple of parking and speeding tickets. Her credit is good. She pays her rent on time. Her car was a college graduation gift from her parents so she has no vehicle debt. Her outstanding student loans are low. She lives in a modest townhouse, one that you'd expect from a twenty-four-year-old teacher. Not a great neighborhood but not a dump. And so far, our surveillance on her house has shown no visits from any of the Minotaurs."

"Sounds pretty squeaky, if you ask me." John tapped his pen on the table, hating to grouse but he'd hoped they could find something about Paula that they could turn over to the authorities.

"Yes, but I didn't mention her bank account."

John stopped the movement of his pen. A hasty glance around proved the others in the room were paying close attention as well.

Josh continued, "In the past month, she's had four cash deposits into her savings account. All less than six thousand dollars, well under the limit so it doesn't tip off anyone's radar at the bank, but there's no evidence of where the money comes from. Then, a week or so after the deposit, she withdraws it."

"Payoffs?" John asked, leaning forward, his forearms resting on the table.

"That'd be my guess," Bray said, drawing John's attention over to him. "According to what Lucy told you, Paula has been going to Canada for several months, ostensibly under the guise of music festivals and concerts.

"Hell, this is like déjà vu," Clay said. When John tilted his head in silent question, Clay explained. "My fiancée is a musician—a violinist. She not only plays in an orchestra but also in a Celtic band that travels to some festivals locally and in Canada. That's where we first got involved with the International Drug Task Force and the Minotaurs."

"Fuckin' hell, so this really isn't anything new for

you all?" John shook his head before turning to Mace. "I'm not stupid enough to think that we're going to shut down an entire network of outlaw biker gangs, but how do we keep this out of our backyard? I mean, Paula works at a local elementary school!"

Mace held his gaze for a long moment then slowly nodded. "And that right there is what lets me know you fit with us as a Keeper."

John's brow furrowed but he remained silent, feeling the heavy weight of Mace's stare while the smiles were coming from the others. Not knowing what Mace was referring to, he waited.

Mace leaned forward, now mimicking John's posture. "You want Lucy safe. We get that. We do, too. But I wondered if this was only about a woman you care for. But with that statement about our backyard and the elementary school, that tells me that your concern goes beyond just you. That it extends to a broader scope of protection."

John slowly let the held air from his lungs out, feeling as though he'd just passed a major test but hadn't realized he was being quizzed.

Mace continued as though he hadn't just laid a world of good onto John. "Drugs? Can she get them across the border without being sniffed out?"

"What about guns?" Bray asked. "Lucy said there were guns on the table beside the drugs."

"The amount of drugs she saw could have been for the Minotaurs' recreational use instead of for Paula to transport," Tate said. "But the guns she observed also seem to be what they would have carried for their own use as well."

"What if she just provides an account to run money through?" John asked. "I've been thinking about what Lucy said about Paula. That she's not wild but likes to act like she is. That she gets off on the idea of going out with a bad boy. Lucy's even intimated that Paula is nice but not always smart. From what I've seen, I'd say that assessment is right."

"Would she be dumb enough to let someone give her cash to deposit and take it back out for them when they needed it?" Walker asked.

Mace turned to Josh. "Dig deeper into her accounts." Looking at John, he added, "Keep Lucy safe. You can let her know we're still investigating Paula, but you can't discuss this with her. I know it's hard, but we don't want her unwittingly getting in harm's way."

He nodded, wondering how he was going to be involved while investigating. The sound of chuckles met his ears, and his gaze shot to the others at the table.

"Most of us met our significant others while investigating. It's not easy, but we've been where you are." Mace's lips quirked upward. "You make it to the other side, you'll know you've got someone worth keeping."

As the others left their chairs at the table to move to their stations, he sat for a moment, taking it all in. His mind filled with Lucy, and he knew one thing for sure— she was worth everything.

On his way to her house after work, he dialed a number he'd programmed into his phone but hadn't used yet. As soon as the line connected, he wondered if the person would even remember him.

"Um… Cam? This is John Roster. I'm not sure if you'll remember, but we met and talked at the—"

"John! Yes, of course, I remember you. We met at the USO in Atlanta. How are you?"

"I'm doing good, really good. I have a new job and wanted to thank you for your encouragement. It turns out my grandfather has a friend who works for a security company. I wasn't too sure they'd want me, but I took the chance and got the job."

"John, that's amazing. I'm really happy for you, man."

"So, how are things with you?"

"Couldn't be better. Made it to Hope City and got a job as an investigator for the Hope City District Attorney. I'm finally out from behind a desk every day."

"Congratulations, Cam. That's wonderful." He hesitated for a few seconds, then added, "Believe it or not, I'm dating someone. Lucy. She's a teacher."

"A teacher? Is it *the* teacher? The one with the kids' letters?"

Now it was John's turn to laugh. "Yeah. I followed your and Blessing's advice and visited them. It was great, and I'll help out with their field day coming up soon. And best of all, I fell for the teacher."

"I couldn't be happier for you, John. I'm glad you called."

As they said their goodbyes with promises to keep in touch, John's mind wandered back to the hurricane and the USO. He hoped the others were doing well also, but worried in particular about Jaxson. *I need to call him, too.*

But what if my life is coming together and his is crap?
Blowing out a breath, he decided he'd check in with him
soon. *Maybe that's what he needs, to hear that there can be
life after the service is jerked away. And maybe, just maybe,
there'll be someone for him like Lucy.*

"Mighty fine eating, Linda." Gramps had just finished
swallowing a bite of his corn-on-the-cob and smiled
over at Lucy's mom.

"Thank you, Rupert. Mitchell and I are just so glad
to finally meet you and John."

John sat at the wooden table under a large tree in
Lucy's parents' backyard. As soon as Lucy had invited
him and Gramps to their family's picnic, Gramps had
talked about nothing else. *He's been alone, and I'd never
realized how alone until I came home.* Gramps had a few
old buddies but many of them had died or moved to be
with family in their older years. His grandfather would
meet some, like Horace, for a beer, but most of the time,
his arthritis made getting around harder, and his weak-
ening eyesight made him more afraid to drive.

So, with the invitation extended, Gramps had
marked the date on the calendar and looked forward to
the simple event. When John came downstairs, ready to
leave, he'd grinned at the sight of his grandfather
already sitting at the kitchen table, a large watermelon
he'd taken out of the refrigerator sitting in front of him,
impatiently hurrying John along.

John, on the other hand, had been nervous. He

wanted to make a good impression and for her family to like him because if he had his way, he and Lucy would be spending many years together.

By the time they swung by Lucy's house to pick her up, he was a bundle of nerves and wishing he'd brought an extra shirt since he was convinced that he'd sweat through the one he was wearing by the time they arrived. Plus, with Lucy in shorts and a tank-top, his thoughts kept moving to what she looked like naked. *Christ, I'll show up with a boner. That'll make an impression!*

He thanked God that by the time they arrived at the Carringtons' house he'd laughed at the banter between Lucy and Gramps over who was going to have the biggest watermelon. Once there, he discovered Lucy's parents were as calm and laid back as she was.

Quick observation gave evidence that Lucy had gained her chestnut hair, petite frame, and ready smile from her mother. Her dad gave her his dark eyes and his penchant for home projects, although, after a home tour, he'd observed that her dad finished his projects before moving on to the next one.

Her brother, Marty, was two years older than Lucy, worked for a logging company, and was easygoing with an obvious affection for his sister but shared the same frustrations that her father had with her house.

"So, sis, did you ever get those shutters up?"

"Yes, they're up." She grinned widely. "I finally decided on deep hunter green. Oh, and John helped me screw the porch boards in place as well so I won't stub my toes on the loose nails that pop up."

Not wanting to take the credit, John added, "Actually, I showed her how, and she did almost all the work herself."

"That's my girl," Mitchell said. "Once she finally decides on a project, then she learns what she needs to do." He leaned toward John and lowered his voice. "But we're happy she's got someone to share in the tasks. She gets a bit distracted."

"I heard that, Dad."

John wrapped his arm around her shoulders, glad that she had a family that could tease while their affection was obvious.

"John's been working around my house," Gramps added, nodding toward Linda as she slid another piece of pie onto his plate. He looked over at Lucy and grinned, waving his fork in the air. "You ever get finished with your place, you can come over and work on mine with him."

"Oh, I'd like that." Lucy smiled, twisting around to look at John. "Just let me know when."

"Why don't you just hire someone to do it? Why would you want to do it yourself?"

All eyes turned toward Marty's date. He'd brought someone with him to their Memorial Day picnic, but it was easy to see that while he was attentive, the woman meant nothing special to him. Lucy did her best to include Joanne, but it also appeared that Joanne was more interested in the bar she and Marty had talked about hitting after the family picnic.

"I like knowing that I made my house my own," Lucy explained. "I do hire out what I can't handle, but I love to paint and have taught myself how to refinish floors and cabinets, how to tile and grout, and now the porch is perfect."

Joanne twirled her hair and shrugged. "Seems boring to me." Marty shot his date a glare as the others hid their smiles.

John thought about years past when he'd been in Marty's shoes. Granted, he never went to a woman's house to be with their family, but he'd had plenty of dates where the most interesting thing was knowing what would happen when they were alone.

His fingers trailed small circles on Lucy's shoulder while turning his attention to her dad and brother's animated discussion with Gramps about the county's plans for new neighborhoods on land that should remain forested. Since Mitchell, Marty, and Gramps were on the same side of the issue, he didn't have to worry. Instead, he leaned back and enjoyed his surroundings. His belly was full of good food, the conversation flowed easily amongst the gathering, the sun was shining, and the woman he loved was tucked into his side.

Loved? He blinked at the word, his heart skipping a beat as he heard her gentle laughter and watched her eyes twinkle. The scent of her shampoo wafted past, and the feel of her head on his shoulder was a weight he wanted to carry always. Fighting the urge to shout and smile, he remained still while acknowledging what he knew was true. *Hell, yeah... I love her!*

20

"I hate that I won't see you later," Lucy said, her phone pressed between her shoulder and ear as she waited inside her classroom for Mrs. Farthingale to bring her class back from lunch. She was multitasking by taking the call from John while hanging up classwork on the bulletin board.

"Me, too, babe. But each Keeper spends one evening every other week in the headquarters monitoring the security feeds and checking what might come in. This is the first time I've gotten the assignment."

"Is it interesting to watch the security feeds? Are there famous people… oh, yeah, you can't tell me. Never mind." She laughed. "Well, for your sake, I hope it's interesting."

"I've been told it's mostly boring, but it feels good to be taking on more of the responsibilities that the others shoulder."

"I'll miss you, you know. I've gotten rather used to some big guy sleeping with me."

"Oh, yeah? Who's this big guy and do I need to take him out?"

Laughing, she shook her head. "You goof. Go do your super-secret security thing, and I've got to ride herd over twenty-six fifth graders. I'll talk to you tomorrow."

Disconnecting, her smile stayed on her face as she tossed her phone into her purse. Her classroom door opened. Knowing it was too early for her class to arrive, she jerked around to see who had entered. Seeing Paula, she cocked her head to the side, curious to see what she needed.

"Um, hey," Paula said, entering but stopping just inside the door.

She'd seen little of Paula in the weeks since they'd gotten back from Canada, but she'd smiled at her in the hall and across the library during the faculty meeting. But it was harder to pretend that nothing was wrong, so she'd managed to have excuses for not being around her. Of course, that was easier since Paula had not been seeking her out.

"Hi, what's up?"

"I Just thought that I'd pop in and see how you were. I haven't seen much of you recently."

She noticed Paula leaned against the doorframe, her arms crossed in front of her either defensively or protectively, she wasn't sure which. She smiled but continued to hang several pieces of her students' work on the bulletin board. "Oh, you know how the end of the year is. I've arranged for help to come in for our

Field Day and end-of-year party. I'm trying to keep the kids on task as we finish out the year. Once they've had their state assessments, they tend to think the year is over."

"Tell me about it. My third-graders are nuts right now." Paula glanced to the side, then looked back toward Lucy. "I heard Mrs. Farthingale say your soldier was coming in for Field Day. Is that who you got to help?"

"Yes, and the kids are so excited to see him again."

"And… um… she intimated that you two are dating."

Lucy finished with the last work to go on the bulletin board and turned to face Paula. "That's true, we are."

"That seems kind of fast, doesn't it?"

A bark of laughter erupted, and Lucy didn't try to keep the incredulity from her voice. "Fast? Come on, Paula, I can't imagine *you* thinking someone starting to date after knowing each other for a while would be fast." It was a dig, one which she wasn't proud of but felt Paula deserved, nonetheless.

Paula's eyes flashed, and her mouth tightened into a straight line. She looked to the side and huffed before her shoulders slumped and she brought her gaze back to Lucy. "Look, I know things fell apart for us, and I'm really sorry. The truth is that I miss you, Lucy. I guess it's hard for me to believe that you're dating someone, and I didn't even know about it."

Some of the fire fled from Lucy in the face of Paula's obvious discomfort. "Honestly, my relationship with

John is still new, so it's not like I've gone around and blasted it to everyone except you."

Paula attempted a smile, but it still appeared tight. "Well, I'm happy for you. I also stopped by to see if you wanted to have a drink. We could hit one of the restaurants near me. It's been a long time since we've had a glass of wine together and just chatted. But you probably have something going on with John, don't you?"

It was on the tip of her tongue to decline, but she hesitated. *Maybe Paula is trying to make amends. Maybe she's seen the light and an outlaw biker is not who she wants to be around. Maybe I could be a good influence if she's still not sure.* Smiling again, she said, "As it turns out, he's busy tonight. I'd love a glass of wine, so thanks for the invite."

Paula smiled, the first one that reached her eyes since she'd stopped in for a chat. Pushing off from the doorframe, she nodded. "Okay, good. I don't have to stay late today, so we can meet at the little place around the corner from me at about five." She lifted her hand in a little wave and turned to walk back down the hall.

Before Lucy had a chance to consider Paula's change in attitude or her invitation, she could hear her class returning and stepped to the doorway to greet them as they came in.

"Do you miss it?"

John sat with Bray, who'd volunteered to be his first

surveillance partner after most of the others had left for the day. Looking up as Bray settled into a seat in front of a bank of monitors, he cocked his head to the side. "Miss it?"

"The Forces? Your team?"

With someone else, John might be tempted to offer a flippant answer, but Bray came from the same background. He sighed as he leaned forward, his forearms resting on his knees. For a moment he dropped his chin and studied his boots as he pondered the question. Finally, he lifted his head and pinned his friend with a direct gaze. "Yeah... sometimes. My team had been together for a while, and we could anticipate each other's movements. Hell, we could almost finish each other's sentences. They were brothers. and being forced to leave was like having my damn arm ripped from my body."

Bray pinched his lips together and nodded. "I hear you. I know you think I can't relate because I left willingly, but I can. I used to lay awake at night, so scared I'd made a mistake I thought I'd piss myself. Never had such self-doubt."

"I heard about what happened. Man, you were the medic when your team got hit. Bray, no one could ever second guess that you needed a break before *you* broke."

"I was a lucky fuck though. I was contacted by Mace. He was friends with my former commander. He told me his vision and how much he needed a medic among his Keepers. He assured me that I would be mostly security and investigations like the others, but just like Drew is our pilot, I'd be able to use my medic skills when needed."

"Seems like we both ended up in a good place." John rubbed his chin, a smile playing about his lips.

"Hell, yeah. Mace is picky about who he employs, so the group is tight. He has no time for egos or someone who's out to play civilian-soldier. He only wants those of us who can do the job and understand the Keeper mentality."

An easy peace settled inside, and John grinned as he nodded toward the screens. "So, you ready to teach me the task of monitoring surveillance feeds?"

Bray grinned in return and then pointed out the various screens in front of them. "We don't man the security twenty-four-seven. For a few of our clients, mostly government officials who want an added layer or clients that can afford our level of security, it's the systems Mace provides. We farm out some of our security feeds to companies that Mace deems worthy who specialize in watching screens continually. We also monitor local law enforcement chatter. Mace wants to make sure that we know what's going on in our own backyard, so to speak." He chuckled. "That's how he met Sylvie. We stepped in to help her when the local police didn't take her seriously when her son witnessed a murder. There was no body, but Mace was convinced he was telling the truth."

"No shit?" John shook his head in disbelief.

"Seriously, that's how they met." Bray turned back to the monitors. "Mace likes to have someone here at night, especially if we have someone in the field. So, that's why we each take a night every other week. Now, for our active investigations, we'll have some surveillance in place and can go back to review when needed."

"Like Lucy's place?"

"Yep." Bray pointed to a screen. "This is on her place." He pointed to another one, adding, "And here is Paula's. These others are more current investigations or newer security clients."

John leaned closer to the screen and stared at the front of Paula's townhouse. "I thought her place would be trendier. She lives in a decent townhouse but the location is crap. What's that tall chain-link fence connected to?"

"There's a storage facility on the other side of her back alley—"

He swung his head around. "Seriously? Do you think she's—"

"I know what you're thinking. Josh looked but she doesn't have a storage unit there. Neither does anyone else associated with the Minotaurs that he can find. Even though she's got easy access from her back door, she's never gone over there since we've been monitoring her, although that's only been a short while. Josh is cross-referencing anyone who had a storage unit to see if they might be a front for the Minotaurs. Since we've had an eye on Paula, Griz has only shown up once." Bray leaned back, his eyes on the screen. "I've been in that area of town before. That place might be crappy now, but I think that neighborhood is going to be revitalized over the next several years, so the owner might do well. Either sell or raise the rent."

Curious, he asked, "What about you? Rent or own?"

Bray grinned. "I bought a house last year. On a bay property so I can get my kayak out. Are you still with your grandfather?"

Nodding, he shifted to a more comfortable position in his chair so that when he glanced at the screens, he didn't need the peripheral vision in his left eye to see them. "Yeah. I've been working on his place, fixing things and making improvements. I'm not ready to make any decisions now. He needs some help and I've also spent most nights with Lucy."

"Sounds good and definitely sounds like you don't need to run out and buy a piece of property now. Save your money, work on your grandfather's place, and see where things go with Lucy."

"Things go the way I hope, she'll be with me permanently and then we can decide where to live and how best to help Gramps."

Bray grinned, shaking his head. "Damn, you didn't waste any time, did you?"

Shrugging, he said, "You know, I realize it seems fast, but when it's right, you just know it." Holding Bray's gaze, he cocked his head to the side. "What about you?"

Bray shook his head. "Man, there's just too much of this goodness to go around. Can't see holding it all for one woman."

"You're so full of shit." Laughing, John turned back to the monitors but not before he caught what he could have sworn was a wistful look on Bray's face.

After a while, Bray stood and stretched, cracking his neck as he twisted side to side. "You want some coffee?"

John nodded and stood, ready to move around and take a break. Glancing back at the screen with a view of the front and side of Paula's townhouse, he leaned closer, then blinked at the sight of the vehicle parking close by. "What the hell is she doing there?"

21

Lucy drove up to Paula's house earlier than scheduled but figured she could kill time by planning her next trip to the hardware store. Parking to the side of the end-unit townhouse, she was struck, not for the first time, how glad she was to have her house in the woods instead of a townhouse in the city.

Paula's rental backed to an alley that was next to a storage facility, but Paula claimed the location that was near several restaurants and bars made it perfect. She had a few neighbors in the other townhouses, but they were elderly and kept to themselves. Paula would laugh when she said her neighbors were hard of hearing so they didn't care what music she played and couldn't see very well so they didn't know if she brought somebody home for the night.

She sighed heavily. The excitement she used to feel when visiting Paula was gone. *And the odds of it coming back are slim.* Closing her eyes for a moment, she cast her mind back in time. The first time she'd met Paula a couple of years ago was when the principal asked her to be one of the new teacher's mentors. *"I think Paula will make a wonderful teacher, Lucy, but you would be a steady influence and are close to her age."*

In truth, she was five years older than Paula, had just bought her fixer-upper house, and was mired in projects to accomplish. In many ways, they couldn't have been more different. But maybe that was why they clicked. Paula got Lucy to go out more and have some fun. Lucy convinced Paula that lesson plans needed to be written on time and Monday morning hangovers needed to be left back in college. Looking up at Paula's house, she now wondered if their friendship had been more of a convenience rather than a true melding of hearts. *So why am I here?* A ready answer didn't come, but she figured a chance to see if there was anything left of a friendship over a glass of wine wasn't a bad thing.

The sound of a vehicle coming down the street met her ears and she turned to see Paula's small sedan approach. Lifting her hand to wave, she was surprised when Paula turned short of her street and parked off to the side. Climbing out, Paula jogged over to the side of the storage facility office and waited until a man came from around the corner. She reached into her bag and pulled out an envelope, folded it in half, and poked it through one of the openings in the chain-link fence. The man accepted the envelope and the two of them stood for a moment while he opened it and peered down, his fingers riffling through whatever was inside.

Eyes wide, Lucy wondered what she was seeing, and her active imagination went into overdrive. The man looked up at Paula and appeared to speak harshly. Lucy rolled her window down to see if she could hear what they were saying, but only a few words were discernible. From what she could tell, he didn't think it was enough of whatever it was, and Paula was insisting it was all she had.

Sucking in her lips, she continued to watch as Paula whirled around and hustled to her car. Once inside, she drove the rest of the block and parked to the side of her townhome. Alighting, she walked quickly to her back door and disappeared.

Lucy sat for a moment, blinking as her gaze swung back to the man. He'd pulled out his phone and was talking as he walked back into the office. Lucy looked at the time on her phone. It was still fifteen minutes before they were supposed to meet, but she decided to find out what was happening. If Paula needed help, she wanted to know. If Paula was insistent on going her own way, then Lucy decided there was no reason to have dinner. Their friendship would truly have changed.

Throwing open her door, she marched to the front door and rang the bell. It took a moment, but Paula opened it, her chin jerking back slightly as Lucy stood on the front step, her hands on her hips.

"What's going on, Paula?" Without waiting for an invitation, she pushed her way inside and turned to face her.

"What do you mean?" Paula's gaze shot from Lucy to outside the still open front door, down to the floor, and back up to Lucy's face again.

"You handing over something to that man at the storage facility."

A gasp followed by Paula's eyes widening gave Lucy all the information she needed to know that something was going on.

"It's... I was just... I have a storage unit there."

"And you make payments through the fence and then argue with the man?"

"Um... I was in a hurry and didn't want to take the time to go inside to pay."

"You're lying."

Paula opened her mouth but said nothing before she took a step backward, closed the door, and leaned against it. She dragged in a heavy breath before letting it out, her shoulders slumping at the same time. "Why are you here, Lucy? Why are you really here?"

A low, sad tenor was in Paula's voice. Lucy's posture mimicked hers as her shoulders slumped and her purse plopped onto the floor. Lifting her hands to the side, palms up, she shrugged. "Truthfully? I suppose I'm here to see if our friendship was real or just one of convenience. The past couple of years, we've enjoyed each other's company at work, but when we went out, it was usually to do something you wanted to do. We never really just sat around and talked. I hadn't thought about that until recently. You wanted to go bar hopping, I'd go along, which in hindsight makes no sense. While we enjoyed some of the same things, that was never my scene. But I let you convince me that I needed to loosen up and be more fun when in reality fun for me was working on my house, something you never understood. I don't think it was until that night at Moose's and then when you ditched me in Canada that I truly understood that our friendship wasn't based on a true togetherness."

The silence filled the space of Paula's small entryway, threatening to choke off the oxygen. She refused to look away, and finally saw evidence of some remorse when moisture gathered in Paula's eyes and she blinked rapidly.

Scrunching her mouth to the side as her chin wobbled, Paula nodded slowly. "I was nervous to move to a new area, start a new job, not know anybody. When the principal first mentioned that I was going to get a mentor, I was sure she was going to give me to some old teacher who'd been around for decades. When she gave me to you, I thought I'd hit the jackpot. You're well-liked by the other staff and kids and parents. You're fun and energetic. And on top of that, you're just really nice. But I wasn't ready to settle down, still loving the life I had in college, and I looked at you like any other college friend I'd had. Someone to go to bars with. A wingman. Someone to talk about our sexcapades with." She shook her head. "I was stupid. I should have realized a long time ago that that just wasn't you. And that you were waiting for me to grow the fuck up."

Those words were not what she expected to come out of Paula's mouth. Pressing her lips together, she finally sighed. "My mother used to tell me that there were people who came into our lives at different times for different reasons. Some to stay for a long time and others more briefly. But they all had the potential to touch my life, help me learn, help me grow. I don't regret the times we had together, Paula. And I'd really like to help you because I feel like you're in trouble. If you're not and don't need me, then I'll walk away and we can remain good, professional coworkers. But I've seen you change over the last month, and it doesn't seem like a good change. Who you're hanging out with, the dark circles under your eyes, and what I just saw outside."

Paula lifted a hand and swiped under her nose, sniffing. "I just got myself in a bit of a mess, that's all. But I'm taking care of it and will be fine. And while I appreciate your offer, what I'm dealing with needs to be handled by me and me alone. I don't want you to get involved."

"If you're in trouble or danger, let's get help," Lucy pleaded.

Before Paula had a chance to respond, the rumble of a motorcycle was heard coming closer. Paula's eyes widened, her head jerking toward the back of her townhouse. "Shit! He must've called Griz!"

Lucy grabbed Paula's shoulder. "What's happening? What's going on?"

"You've got to get out of here. You can't be here when he comes. You've got to go!" Paula's hand twisted the doorknob, but she peeked out the slender window first, a gasp fleeing her mouth. "Shit!"

Unable to see what Paula was looking at, Lucy cried out, "What?"

Paula grabbed Lucy's hand and dragged her to a door under the staircase leading to the second floor.

"Get into the basement! Whatever you do, whatever you hear, stay quiet! You can't be found here!"

"Paula—"

"No, there's no time! Listen, I didn't have all the money to pay the guy at the storage facility so he called Griz to see what's going on. It's fine, I'll take care of it. But if you're found here, things could get ugly. And by ugly, I mean for both of us! So go down there, stay quiet, and let me deal with this!"

Lucy looked down into the dark basement, the stairs illuminated by a single bulb halfway down.

"Go! It's the only way to keep you safe!" Paula's eyes were filled with panic, that emotion finally kicking in with Lucy.

She heard the door shut behind her as she raced down the wooden stairs, her heartbeat pounding to the rhythm of her footsteps. Just as she neared the bottom, the light went out and she stumbled, barely managing to right herself before she splattered onto the concrete floor.

Dim daylight was still coming in through two small, dirty windows at the back of the basement wall near the ceiling, and she hurried over toward them. As her eyes acclimated to the light, she looked around. A few boxes sat in a corner, appearing to have been here for a long time, probably before Paula moved in. Movement shot along the wall toward the boxes, and she clapped her hand over her mouth to still the squeal that threatened to erupt at the sight of a mouse.

Voices were heard from above but she had no idea who was there or what was being said. *Christ, what have*

I stumbled into? She considered going back up the stairs to listen at the door but quickly dismissed that notion. *If the door opens, I have no chance of getting away.*

Tiptoeing over to the windows, she looked to see if there was an escape route through them. They were small, the townhouse built before the regulations that determined the size of windows for a basement. She was sure she was petite enough to make it through if she could get them open, but there was nothing available for her to stand on other than the boxes that she knew were hiding mice.

Shoving her fears of rodents to the side, she pushed the box toward the back wall, wincing at the scraping sound it made on the concrete. Finally, standing on the box, she could just barely reach the window latch. She pushed and shoved but it wouldn't budge. Blowing out a breath, she jumped as a shadow passed the window. Crouching down, she peered through the grime and thought it was the man that Paula had talked to from the storage facility. Moving down off the box very slowly, she moved into the shadows, out of sight.

Blowing out a long breath, she wondered what to try next. *Hopefully, Griz will just leave, and Paula will let me know the coast is clear.*

She tiptoed away from the window, creeping toward the bottom of the stairs. Indecision flooded her as the voices from upstairs grew louder. The memory of her purse dropping to the floor by the front door hit her, and she snapped her hand to her pocket, breathing a sigh of relief at the feel of her phone.

Pulling it out, she saw she'd missed five calls, all from John. Just then, a message came in.

Paula's house under surveillance. On our way.

Sucking in a hasty breath, she glanced back up the stairs as though someone was going to catch her on the phone before she typed out a return message.

Griz upstairs with Paula. I'm hiding in basement. Man outside in back.

Another message came in.

Stay where you are. Police on their way. Love you... stay safe. Almost there.

She blinked at the words, her heart pounding, not sure what was hitting her the hardest—that he was almost here or that he loved her. Clutching the phone in her hands and pressing it tightly to her chest, she knew. *He loves me.* Any other man, that might be a throwaway phrase, but not John.

"What the fuck is wrong with you, bitch? You think you can just walk away from me? You fuckin' owe me the rest of the money!"

"I gave it to him. I gave everything that's been deposited to me. I swear, Griz, I can show you my bank statement. Two thousand dollars was put in, and that's what I just gave him."

"Five fuckin' thousand dollars was supposed to been put in your account."

"It wasn't," Paula cried.

Lucy winced at the sound of something crashing above her. Praying it was just a chair and not Paula herself, she tiptoed halfway up the stairs, not knowing how to help. John had said the police were on their way and she squeezed her eyes shut. *Please, God, let them get here fast!*

"No!" Paula screamed, and the sound of scuffling was heard, then all went quiet.

Her heart dropped to her stomach and Lucy raced up the stairs. It was rash to hurl toward a dangerous unknown, but she couldn't stay in hiding while someone was being hurt. With her ear pressed to the door, she sucked in a breath as her hand landed on the knob.

It didn't turn. *I'm locked in?* Jiggling the door, she felt it move then catch again. *Dammit!* Continuing to jerk the stuck door knob back and forth, it finally turned, and she flung the door open. Bolting from the basement, she screamed, seeing Paula on the floor, eyes closed and blood running from her nose. Dropping next to Paula, the air rushed out as she spied Paula's eyes fluttering open.

"I'll call an ambulance." She jerked her phone from her pocket again, but the front and back doors were flung open at the same time, several uniformed police officers entering, weapons drawn.

"We need an ambulance!" she shouted. "The man who hurt her just left, but there's another guy out there!"

One of the officers dropped to her side, immediately assisting Paula, saying, "We got the men."

A growl at the front door sounded, and she looked up to see John storm in, jaw tight, eyes flashing as they landed on her. As he stalked forward, she leaped to her feet and rushed into his arms. "I'm okay. I'm okay."

"You fuckin' weren't okay. You were in a fuckin' basement with a fuckin' maniac drug dealer right fuckin' above you." His voice was still a growl, but a smile slipped over her face at his colorful although accurate description. His arms had banded tightly around her, lifting her slightly so their hearts beat next to each other.

She leaned back to peer into his eyes, the haunting specter of fear still visible. Cupping his face, she held him close. "I wasn't okay, but now I'm in your arms, John, and we're perfect."

22

All the missions he'd gone on. All the rescues he'd participated in. All the successes he'd had as a member of the Special Forces. Nothing meant as much to John as the feel of Lucy in his arms.

As soon as he'd seen her pull up to Paula's house, fear had spread throughout him. That sixth sense that had saved him and his teammates so often had him shout to Bray that he was heading to Paula's house. With Josh at LSI to monitor the cameras and provide backup, Bray accompanied him as they raced into town, making the thirty-minute trip in only twenty. While Bray drove, he'd continued to watch the security feed on his tablet.

When Lucy had stepped inside Paula's front door, he knew he'd made the right decision in trying to get to her, not trusting Paula at all. Watching as Griz rode in on his bike before heading straight to Paula's door, John had felt his body tighten with anxiety, knowing Lucy was still in there.

Mace, on the line with Bray, had assured them he'd called for the police and the task force. Just as they arrived, Bray jerked his vehicle to a halt, calling out his recognition of someone from the drug task force. John hadn't waited to talk to anyone at the sight of Griz's motorcycle still parked on the side street. He'd raced toward the front of Paula's house with Bray on his heels. When they'd rounded the corner, Griz was handcuffed, surrounded by law enforcement along with another handcuffed man.

Bypassing them all, John had raced up Paula's steps and into her house, seeing Lucy kneeling on the floor. He'd growled, unable to halt his progress until he had her in his arms, pressed against his chest.

Now, she was staring up at him, assuring him that she was fine. *Christ, Almighty, I never want to feel that helpless ever again.*

"She hid me in the basement. She didn't tell him that I was here," Lucy said, her gaze now on Paula as they loaded her onto a gurney.

Paula looked up, one eye swelling and fingerprint bruises around her throat. "Lucy?"

At the sound of her name, Lucy squirmed to have John let her down. He acquiesced, although reluctantly. She moved past the EMT and leaned over Paula, taking her hand.

"I'm sorry," came the hoarse whisper. "I never meant for any of this to happen. I certainly never meant for any of this to touch you." Looking beyond Lucy, Paula caught John's eye. "Take care of her."

Stepping closer, he put his hands on Lucy's shoulders. He choked back the words of anger and guilt he wanted to heap upon Paula and instead just nodded. "I will."

As the EMTs rolled Paula out, Lucy twisted her head around to look up at him. "What's going to happen to her?"

"I don't know, babe. I don't know her level of involvement. But as soon as we saw Griz was in the area, the International Drug Task Force was alerted. They've already been investigating him, and they'll be the ones to talk to her and decide if she's committed any crimes."

As soon as those words left his mouth, Lucy's shoulders slumped, and he wrapped his arms around her back, pulling her into his chest again, offering what comfort he could. "Why did you come over here today?"

"She stopped by my room earlier and said that she missed me. Missed our friendship. Then she invited me to meet her for drinks at a restaurant around the corner. I got here early and was trying to decide how I felt about everything. If I'd judged her too harshly. Or maybe if our friendship was based more on convenience and not true feelings. Anyway, I was sitting in my car and saw her pull up and stop at the storage facility. She got out, but instead of going through the gate and into the office, she just walked to the fence where she waited until a man came out. I saw her pull out a thick envelope and shove it through the fence. He took it, looked through it, and it appeared they were having not-happy words. It was like something out of a movie or TV crime show. While I couldn't be sure, I was almost certain that I was watching some kind of handoff or payoff."

Now, she lifted her cheek from his chest and leaned her head back so she could peer up into his face. "Oh, John, I got so angry. She drove to the back of her house and went in, and I climbed out of my vehicle and stomped straight up to her front door. Righteous indignation was pouring from me, and I was ready to tell her our friendship had no meaning. Now, I'm so embarrassed."

"Lucy, babe, you've got no reason to be embarrassed. While we don't know all the details, it's pretty obvious that Paula was involved with a known criminal who's part of an organization that runs drugs, guns, money laundering, and who knows what else. I'm just sorry as fuck that she was trying to hang on to your friendship at a time when she needed to protect you by staying away."

Bray walked over, his hand landing on John's shoulder while he looked at Lucy. "Hey, Lucy. I'm Bray, one of John's coworkers. How're you doing?"

"Damn, I should have asked if she needed you," John said, grimacing. Seeing Lucy's crinkled forehead, he added, "Bray is a medic."

She smiled and shook her head. "It's nice to meet you, but no, I'm fine. Really. A bit overwhelmed with the last hour's events, but that's all."

Bray offered a chin lift to go along with his smile. Turning his attention back to John, he said, "Mace said once Lucy has given her contact information to the

Task Force, then we're good to go. They'll talk to her sometime soon but not today."

It only took a few minutes for Lucy to talk to the agent after Bray led her and John over, giving a preliminary explanation of why she was there and what she'd seen. The agent thanked her and said he'd come by in the next few days to take her formal statement. John wrapped his arm around her shoulder and led her down the sidewalk. They stopped at Bray's truck, and he turned to clasp his friend's hand. "I can't thank you enough, man."

Bray waved him off. "Hell, there hasn't been that much excitement on surveillance in a long time. Normally, it's boring as shit."

Rolling his eyes, he laughed. "Next time, I hope it is boring as shit."

"Don't worry about your vehicle. I can come to pick you up tomorrow morning." Bray inclined his head slightly toward Lucy, holding John's gaze. Catching his friend's silent question, he nodded to be picked up at Lucy's house in the morning. No way was he going to leave her side tonight.

Bray grinned, nodded, then reached out and kissed Lucy's forehead. "I'm glad you're okay. Next time we have a Keeper get-together, have this guy bring you."

John then pulled Lucy back into his side as they walked to her car. "I'll have to scoot the driver's seat back so I can fit in behind the steering wheel, but I'm driving, sweetheart."

She handed him the keys and laughed. "If I wasn't

having such an adrenaline crash, I'd fight you over who could drive my car."

On the drive back to her house, he'd worried about her state of mind, but now that the crisis was over and Griz was in custody, her relief was obvious.

That night, lying in her bed, naked in the aftermath of making love with legs tangled, chests pressed together, and her head on his shoulder, he peered into her eyes as his finger traced over her jaw. "What would you say if I told you that I want to stay?"

Lifting a brow, she smiled. "What would you say if I told you that I don't want you to leave?"

A deep chuckle erupted. "What would you say if I told you that I'm not just talking about tonight?"

"What would you say if I told you that I'd like you to move in with me but I don't want to take you away from Gramps?"

His heart began to pound. "Gramps' house is only ten minutes away from yours."

"My house needs a lot of work." He could hear the tremors in her voice.

"It's a good thing I know how to fix a lot of stuff. Plus, together, we might get more things checked off your to-do list and make your dad happy."

For a moment, neither spoke, silent words and warm emotion filling the space around them. When he could hold back no longer, he asked another question. "What would you say if I told you I love you?" At that, she didn't say anything, her breath seeming to halt in her lungs. "The truth is, I do love you, Lucy. I think I've known for a while, but I don't want to hold back anymore."

She blinked away the moisture gathering in her eyes. "You sent a message today where you said 'love you.'"

"I couldn't stand the idea of you being in danger and I'd never told you. But now you need to hear it from my lips. I." He touched his lips to hers. "Love." He kissed her again, ever so lightly. "You." This time, his kiss was deep, his head angled to delve into her warmth. And it didn't end until they'd made love once more.

John sat at the large table, listening to Mace debrief the group. "James Kinder, otherwise known as Griz, is being held without bail. He's being charged with multiple felonies, but it will be a toss-up as to who gets him first, the U.S. or Canada, considering he's wanted in both countries. One way or the other, he'll be in prison. He's just one small cog in the Hell's Angels and Minotaurs wheel, but at least he won't be a problem anymore."

Mace looked over at John. "I don't know how much Paula will turn over. She's scared and rightly so. But she did admit to her part in what happened. It appears she let Griz talk her into being the middle person for a storage unit to hold some of his personal belongings. He told her that because he was a Canadian citizen he couldn't rent it, and she believed him. She had no idea what was in it—it held stolen weapons. She received cash from a variety of people, deposited it into her bank account, and then weekly gave it to the man at the unit. All under the table, of course. By the time she realized Griz was dangerous, it was too late to refuse him."

"Is she facing jail time?" John asked, his thoughts on Lucy. While Lucy had confessed her conflicted feelings about Paula, he knew she would hate for her to go to jail.

Mace shrugged. "I don't know at this time. Perhaps not, especially if she tells what she knows."

"And the fuckin' Minotaurs?" Clay asked. John recognized the man's face was always set in granite every time they talked about the gang that kidnapped Clay's fiancée. He now understood, knowing his expression was the same.

"Due to our proximity to the Canadian border and our numerous cases that can take us to Canada, the International Drug Task Force has asked us to continue to work with them on a case-by-case basis, so I'm sure we'll run into those fuckers again."

John started to push his chair back, thinking the meeting had ended and anxious to get back to Lucy. She was spending the day with Gramps under the guise of helping his grandfather out, but in truth, Gramps wanted to keep an eye on her, and John had been glad for the suggestion. Before he had a chance to stand, Mace called his name. Looking up, he observed all the other Keepers smiling at him. "Yes?"

"I just wanted to say that your probationary status with Lighthouse Security Investigations is over. Welcome aboard as a full-fledged Keeper."

As the others threw out their congratulations, he

swallowed hard, fighting the lump in his throat. He'd never thought to find another team like the one he had in the Army Special Forces. He'd never thought to find employment that fulfilled his desire to plan and execute missions, knowing at the end of the day he was helping others. He'd never thought he would be able to do this work with his limited vision.

But here he was. A Keeper. And the two people he couldn't wait to tell were at home waiting on him. *The man who helped raise me and the woman of my future.* Gramps and Lucy.

23

"Come on, Bobby, come on, Bridget! You can do it!"

John shouted encouragement for Lucy's students as they ran in the Field Day races. Excitement ran through him as he watched the two work together in the race, the other kids shouting from the sideline. His former teammates wouldn't believe their eyes if they saw him shouting for two kids in a race where they carried an egg in a spoon, careful to not drop the egg before crossing the finish line. *But Blessing would believe it.*

As Bobby and Bridget crossed the line first, he jumped and shouted, clapping along with the rest of the students before smiling at Lucy. For Field Day, the principal relaxed the teachers' dress code, and gorgeous as always, she was in jean capris, a sporty T-shirt, and her cute blue sneakers. Unable to help himself, he picked Lucy up and twirled her around, much to the delight of the kids. She play-slapped his shoulder, rolling her eyes as she laughed. The students crowded around Bobby and Bridget as they ran to the side, congratulations flowing. Leaning down, he whispered, "I always knew your class would be the best at the egg race."

"That's because you've come into the classroom and had them practice!" she whispered in return.

"The principal never said that the kids couldn't practice," he argued, his smile wide. In truth, he'd come to her classroom often, helping students with their assignments, reading with those who still struggled, and sharing some of his stories of other cultures from his time in the military. *And if we occasionally practiced walking around the classroom with an egg in a spoon... well, it always helps to be prepared.*

Mrs. Farthingale came over, her phone in her hand. "I want to get the whole class together, and this time, Ms. Carrington, you need to be in the picture!"

John moved to the side, but the aide shook her head. "Oh, no, you need to be in the picture, too. After all, you've been part of this class for most of the year, even if the first part was as our pen pal."

Grinning, he scooted in close to Lucy at the back of the group, allowing the students to be in the front. After Mrs. Farthingale finished snapping several pictures, he moved to her as Lucy herded the kids together to go inside. "Can you send some of those pictures to me?"

"Of course!" They stood together while he pulled out his phone, and she texted the pictures to him. "Make sure you come in soon for the party. If I know those children in there, they'll make quick work of that food!"

"I will. I just have something I need to do first." He watched as she hurried after Lucy's class, and he bent to his phone, tapping out a group text as he attached one of the pictures.

To Cam, Jaxson, Sebastian, Kyle

It was good for me to visit the class that had sent me letters and thank them. I've stayed involved with them, and now the teacher, Lucy Carrington, is my girlfriend. Blessing was right. Gratitude went a long way to helping me find my own happiness. Hope you all are doing well. Let me hear from you. John

Hitting send, he grinned as he shoved his phone into his pocket and jogged into the classroom, ready to battle the students over a cupcake. And then, at the end of the last school day of the year, he and Lucy would go home. Home to stay.

For the next Long Road Home adventures, click below!
Finding Home by Abbie Zanders
Home Again by Caitlyn O'Leary
Home Front by Cat Johnson
My Heart's Home by Kris Michaels

For more Lighthouse Security Investigations click below!
Lighthouse Security Investigations
by Maryann Jordan
Mace
Rank
Walker
Drew

Blake
Tate
Levi
Clay
Cobb
Bray

Cael

Jaxon

Jayden

Asher

Zeke

Cas

Lighthouse Security Investigations

Mace

Rank

Walker

Drew

Blake

Tate

Levi

Clay

Cobb

Bray

Hope City (romantic suspense series co-developed

with Kris Michaels

Brock book 1

Sean book 2

Carter book 3

Brody book 4

Kyle book 5

Ryker book 6

SEALs

Thin Ice (Sleeper SEAL)

SEAL Together (Silver SEAL)

Undercover Groom (Hot SEAL)

Also for a Hope City Crossover Novel / Hot SEAL...

A Forever Dad

Long Road Home

Military Romantic Suspense

Home to Stay (a Lighthouse Security Investigation crossover novel)

Letters From Home (military romance)

Class of Love

Freedom of Love

Bond of Love

The Love's Series (detectives)

Love's Taming

Love's Tempting

Love's Trusting

The Fairfield Series (small town detectives)

Emma's Home

Laurie's Time

Carol's Image

Fireworks Over Fairfield

Please take the time to leave a review of this book. Feel free to contact me, especially if you enjoyed my book. I love to hear from readers!

Facebook

Email

Website

ABOUT THE AUTHOR

I am an avid reader of romance novels, often joking that I cut my teeth on the historical romances. I have been reading and reviewing for years. In 2013, I finally gave into the characters in my head, screaming for their story to be told. From these musings, my first novel, Emma's Home, The Fairfield Series was born.

I was a high school counselor having worked in education for thirty years. I live in Virginia, having also lived in four states and two foreign countries. I have been married to a wonderfully patient man for forty years. When writing, my dog or one of my four cats can generally be found in the same room if not on my lap.

Please take the time to leave a review of this book. Feel free to contact me, especially if you enjoyed my book. I love to hear from readers!

Facebook
Email
Website

Made in United States
Orlando, FL
19 January 2022

13750939R00153